The Author lives in Thurleigh.

The Cursed Sister
By
Andrew Blair

Copyright 2019

No parts of this publication may be reproduced in any form or by any means.
This story is entirely fictional. Any resemblance to people with similar experiences is entirely coincidental.

Chapter One

London England
1972

Karl Bauman suddenly felt his spirits drop. It wasn't a new sensation as it had been happening for 20 odd years. One moment he would be as happy as could be and the next, for no apparent reason, his mood would suddenly plummet.

At one point, several years before, he had been urged by his wife to visit a psychiatrist. The consultation had taken less than 15 minutes.

"You are having sub-conscious flashbacks Mr. Bauman. Most of the time your conscious mind will not know what triggers them. Millions of men all over the World of a similar age to you have them. I do myself. There is nothing we can do about it. Don't worry. Your mood will lift again in a short time."

Karl looked round him trying to ascertain what had caused it.

He, his son and six of his son's friends were in North London for a pre-season friendly between Bayern Munich and Tottenham Hotspur. It was part of his son's pre-wedding celebrations.

"Are you alright Dad?" asked his son.

"Yes Michael I am ok,"

"Another one of your black-dog moments?"

Karl smiled. It was a private joke between them to refer to his low moods in the way Winston Churchill had.

"Yes but its fine."

His son's best friend Seb leant towards them both and said in a low voice

"I am guessing your Dad is not comfortable with the company."

Karl shuddered but tried to keep a smile on his face. He knew what Seb meant. He had been told what to expect but he had never seen so many orthodox Jews in a small area even in pre-war Germany. Every fifth man seemed to have a skull-cap and ringlets in their hair.

"I think it is more of a problem for you Seb than it is for me. But shut up about it. A lot of them are probably not overjoyed to have their area invaded by Germans."

"To be fair," said Michael. "In all the times I have visited England I have never had a problem about the war. The English always claim to have won it single-handedly, and we will get the Dambusters theme tune tonight, but they seem to care much more about the fact we knocked them out of the World cup."

"I take your point, and I remembered being so surprised about it the first time I visited you in London. But it might be different here. This is the most populated Jewish area in Britain."

Seb laughed.

"Don't worry old man. We will look after you."

Karl rolled his eyes.

"Oh that's so reassuring. Your generation has no idea."

"The past is the past and we are the future Granddad."

Karl suppressed a shudder at the familiar words; words that he had trumpeted at a much younger age than Seb while in the uniform of the Hitler youth. This time Seb had said them as a joke but Karl knew that a lot of young Germans were, quite understandably, tired of apologizing for a war that had been fought before they were born. He forced a smile.

"Yes Seb, I am sure you are but please keep quiet about it right now ok."

They walked up the stairs out of the Seven Sisters tube station while Karl kept looking round to try to find the thing that had triggered his "Black-dog moment". When they reached street level he gave up because it seemed to have past.

"Which way to the ground?" asked Seb.

Karl laughed.

"Well if you are the future God help us. There are thousands of people going left so I would say that is probably the direction the ground is."

Seb smiled.

"Just testing to see if you were on the ball old man."

"Hey we have got some Germans,"

Karl turned to see a group made up of five youngish men and one woman all with Tottenham scarf's round their necks and wrists.

"Hey," shouted one young man good-naturedly. "They have come over for another beating."

Then four of them started singing a song Karl had heard before.

"2 world wars and 1 world cup,

2 world wars and 1 world cup"

The woman scowled at them.

"Alright lads that's enough of that bull-shit. It's enough we are going to stuff them tonight. There is no need to take the piss."

Seb fronted up to the young man who had led the singing.

"In your song you seem to have forgotten 2 years ago in Mexico and the fact the 3rd goal in 1966 didn't cross the line."

"Fuck off, that was miles over the line," said the woman with a laugh.

"And you wouldn't have won in Mexico if you cheating bastards hadn't have poisoned our goal-keeper before the match," said one of the other men.

The banter continued as they walked. Karl enjoyed being in England which was not something he had expected when he had first come in 1960.

When the steel company had sent him he had been nervous but, just fifteen years after the war and five after the end of rationing, he had felt very little antipathy toward him. Some had been a bit cold and some even blanked him. But there was hardly any hatred even from the age group who presumably would have fought and lost loved ones in the war.

At first the comedic way the British referred to the war had angered him but he had come to appreciate that this was the way they handled stressful situations. It wasn't exactly forgiveness but it had allowed them to move on in a way other nations couldn't.

It also helped of course that they had never been occupied by the Germans.

"Are you guys coming to the pub before the game," said one of the English lads.

"Lead on old bean," said Seb in an over-the-top English accent. "It is my boy's stag-do as you English say."

That made Michael the centre of attention and when they got to the pub he was the first to be offered a pint. Karl found himself standing next to the woman.

"Is that your son?" she asked.

He smiled.

"Is it that obvious?"

"Well if there are seven young guys and one old guy on a stag-do it is a good bet the old guy is the grooms Dad."

"I think I was meant to turn the invitation down but my wife insisted I come."

"It was a wise decision. You need to watch him as the lads can get a bit rowdy. They might start lacing his drinks and he won't see the match."

He smiled.

"And my boys might try to prove they can hold their beer better than the English."

She laughed.

"Bring it on and sorry for calling you old."

"It is not a problem and thanks for stopping the song."

She made a face.

"Yea, sorry about that. The English football fan is not known for his sensitivity. What's your name by the way?"

He held out his hand.

"Karl and you are?"

She smiled and shook his hand.

"I am Ingrid."

"Do you often go to the football Ingrid?"

"Don't women go to football in Germany?"

He hesitated not wanting to unwittingly insult her.

"They do but it's…its different."

She laughed.

"You mean they don't go on the piss with a load of single guys most of whom are a lot younger than them?"

He smiled enjoying her bluntness.

"Yes I did mean that. One of them seems of a similar age to you."

"That's Joe and no he is not my husband or boyfriend if that's what you were thinking. He is my older brother."

Karl looked at him. The man was smiling, and was on the edge of the group of young German and English lads, but Karl could see he was not engaging as eagerly as the others.

"You and your brother must be close."

She looked at him with a half-smile on her face.

"If you pry anymore it will be one of those awkward moments former enemies sometimes have."

"Ah I see. Your parents were killed in the war."

"Yes,"

"The Blitz I suppose?"

"Yes,"

"I am very sorry,"

"It's ok. I know our bombers killed thousands of your people even when the war was all but over."

"That's true but of the people here I am the only one old enough to have fought in the war."

She smiled but he could sense the pain. In another time, in another life, he had not been so sensitive to people's feelings.

"Were you in the Luftwaffe?"

"No,"

"Then I will forgive you if you buy me a pint,"

He smiled.

"That is very generous. Would you have forgiven me if I had been?"

She smiled back.

"Then it would have taken two pints,"

He brought everyone a drink. The trip was proving very expensive but he was a wealthy man and he was enjoying the break much more than he had expected.

As he walked to the ground with the group he reflected on this change. In the aftermath of Germanys defeat he had, like his comrades, been very bitter. He spent years meeting these veterans, planning revenge, still giving Heil Hitlers, and raising money to keep old colleagues safe from prosecution.

In a way this last had caused the change. He had risen to the top managerial level in the company but this determination to get to the top was, in part, driven by his desire to help his radical ex-Nazi's. He had then set up his own, very profitable business. It meant though that, unlike a lot of his comrades, he had travelled and got a different perspective.

He remembered on that first visit to England he had gone to see Manchester City play. In goal for them was the German ex-prisoner-of-war Bert Trautmann.

Karl knew about Trautmann. He had never met him or served in the same unit but they had been on a similar journey. They had both joined the Hitler youth as young boys and made the same oaths of loyalty to the Reich and Adolf Hitler: oaths that were until death.

Karl knew that before Trautmann could be released by the British they had to be convinced that he had been "De-Nazified". Karl had gone to the ground considering him a traitor. 90 minutes later he had come out with a very different view.

Trautmann was a cult hero and not just with City fans. A few years earlier he had played the last 12 minutes of the English F. A. Cup final with a broken neck.

Trautmann, like him, had been indoctrinated with the Nazi creed from the age of 10. He would have grown up to view Hitler as almost a God; a God he would obey any order from and a God he would willingly die for.

He would have hated the English because he had been ordered to hate the English and he would have killed them for the same reason. And now, just fifteen years later, he was one of the most popular sportsmen in England.

It said a lot for the English of course, and of the healing power of sport, but Karl had realized that this wouldn't have been enough. Trautmann himself would have had to have changed. He would have had to truly accept that what he had been taught from childhood was all lies.

Karl never had, not really. And nor had the majority of his comrades. Hitler had been dead for fifteen years, although many denied even that, but they were still fiercely loyal to him.

But then Karl stepped back and looked at his upbringing like Trautmann obviously had. And then the whole façade that had been his life disintegrated as easily as if he was punching through paper.

It was like a religious awakening. Hitler was not some Messiah who had been sent to save Germany; he was a power-crazed lunatic who had left millions of his countrymen dead and German cities in ruins. He had taken the youth of a nation, brainwashed them, and sent them out to commit atrocities across Europe.

In a way it had been devastating. He had seen himself as an honorable warrior dutifully carrying out orders. If they were deemed necessary by Adolf Hitler, savior of Germany, he would gladly carry them out.

Now he saw Adolf Hitler had turned him into a Monster.

But that realization had also been liberating. He was now free of him and he could be a better man: a good man.

Actually it felt like he had been reborn. He suppressed most memories of his war days and the ones he couldn't his brain seemed to register like a movie; like it wasn't him.

They reached the ground. There were a considerable number of German fans around the away end and many more English fans taunting them behind a line of policemen on horses. It was mostly good-natured, and the Bayern fans were giving some back, but Karl knew it could possibly turn violent at some stage.

"Right you Krauts," said the woman. After we have thrashed you we will meet you here. Then we will go to the pub to give the bride-groom a proper send off."

The young Germans cheerfully agreed. As the English moved away the woman smiled at him.

"Are you coming drinking later old man or are you going home to bed early?"

She had a quite prominent birthmark on her right cheek but still looked quite attractive with her long brown hair, white football shirt and jeans. Among the men she looked confident but Karl thought he sensed some sadness and even loneliness. He smiled at her.

"I will be there young lady."

The others mocked him about the exchange when they got into the ground.

"She is up for it old man," said Seb.

"Don't worry Karl, what happens in London stays in London," said another.

Karl laughed it off.

"I can see how, if she wanted anyone, it would be me rather than one of you immature kids but I think she was only being friendly."

But later, in the pub, he wondered if there was indeed a spark of interest.

Bayern had won the match by a disputed penalty but, as it was a pre-season friendly no one seemed to care. The pub was packed and was also illegally open as it was past 11 pm. Several young girls had joined the group and were taking a keen interest in the young Germans. Karl and Ingrid were pushed to the margins.

"I think us oldies are surplus to requirements Karl."

He smiled.

"I know what you mean but you are being very unfair by bracketing yourself in the same age-group as me."

"I am considerably older than those girls, one of whom seems to be taking an unhealthy interest in your soon-to-be-married son."

Karl looked over to see a young blonde girl, who looked about nineteen, sitting very close to Michael with her hand on his lap. From the expression on his son's face his fiancée back in Munich was not foremost in his mind.

He smiled at Ingrid

"Well it is a stag-do"

"Don't you mind?"

"Well I would prefer him not to sleep with her but as long as he takes precautions I can't really see any harm in it."

"How very Bohemian of you. Are all Germans so free and easy about sex?"

He paused realizing that he was at a crossroads. From the smile on her face Ingrid realized it too. He decided to ignore the safe boring route.

"Not all are. But some of us who have seen how fragile life is understand that you have to fully enjoy the good things that come into your life."

"Even if that means cheating on your wife?"

He smiled.

"My son is not married yet."

She smiled back.

"I was not talking about your son Karl."

He hesitated. This was not a scenario he had envisaged when he agreed to come on the trip. It was also probably not one that his wife had envisaged when she urged him to come either.

"As it is with my son. I don't think a one night stand in a foreign city will endanger my marriage."

She looked at him and then over to where Michael was now kissing the girls neck.

"I think it is good parenting Karl. He is going to sleep with her anyway. So it is better that you just caution him not to bring any nasty surprises back to his bride, either in a few days or a few months. I will get us another beer."

He watched her walk to the bar and noticed she had a slight limp. He realized she was still making her mind up. He also now realized what attracted her to him. He had suspected it anyway but her words had confirmed it. She saw him as a Father figure.

It was far from unusual. A German bomb had robbed her of her parents when she must have been less than ten-years-old. She would have lived with distant family members, who probably didn't want her, or in massively over-stretched orphanages.

There were millions like this across the World. This woman would not have been born when, in a foreign city several hundred miles away, Adolf Hitler became chancellor of Germany. Who could possibly have thought that that event in 1933 would lead to this sad, possibly damaged, girl considering having sex with an older man in 1972.

It had happened to him several times before, all with women about this age and in several different countries. He knew women were attracted to this post-1960 Karl Bauman. He was dignified, kind and polite. At first it had been an act but now it was who he was.

Sometimes he took them up on the offer and sometimes he didn't. It pretty much depended on their emotional state. Once in Berlin he had gone back to a hotel with a woman who had had too much to drink. She had ended up crying hysterically as she described watching her Mother being raped and killed by Russian soldiers.

He didn't envisage any such problems with Ingrid. She would have had a traumatic upbringing but being orphaned in

1945 London was vastly preferable to being so in 1945 Berlin. She would have felt alienated from other women, and even her own age group, but she had found a degree of happiness with her brother and his friends.

Although she was drinking tonight her clear skin did not indicate long-term alcohol abuse. She looked healthy, fit and strong which meant she looked after herself, which meant she had some self-respect, which in turn meant she was unlikely to end up sobbing in Karl's arms after sex.

When she came back with the drinks he instinctively knew she had made up her mind to sleep with him. She smiled and sat down close to him.

"I think it will have to be your place Karl. I live with my brother and he might get a bit funny about it."

"That's ok. I have an understanding hotel. Will your brother be upset?"

"It won't be a problem. We live our own lives?"

"But I suspect me being German is a problem for him. Will he be angry with you?"

"A little but you don't have to worry about it. He doesn't hate Germans but I think you can understand him not being over-the-moon about one of them screwing his sister."

"Yes I can understand that."

They left soon after. Karl took Michael aside and told him to be careful with the girl. Ingrid had gone to the toilet while Karl told his group he was going home to sleep. He had planned it this way because he didn't want ribald comments from the Germans which might enrage the brother. Ingrid joined him outside five minutes later.

Chapter Two

His hotel was only a mile away and they decided to walk. They talked mainly about football and Karl found her surprisingly knowledgeable. He teased her.

"But now I think the German football team is much better than the English."

She smiled.

"Well that's the Germans for you; always so bloody efficient at whatever they do. No rebels or individuals in the team. Everyone singing from the same hymn sheet" She gave him a sardonic grin. "Strong leadership and everyone following orders"

He looked at her and smiled although the reference to the famous Nuremberg trials plea struck a raw nerve.

"Ouch. You do have a point though. Blindly following orders does seem a National trait. We can only hope that in the future the leader giving the orders is a good person. You are an interesting Lady."

"Interesting! Oh great. How very unsexy. I should have pulled a French man."

He laughed thoroughly enjoying her company.

"I mean that there is more to you than meets the eye. You try to fit in with your brother and his friends. You appear to drink as much as they do but I suspect that is a false impression. You carry a pack of cigarettes around with you but I have never seen you smoke. And no disrespect to your friends but I doubt they could have nailed the classic German characteristics as you just did."

She looked at him a bit ruefully.

"What can I say? I am a spy and obviously not a very good one."

He laughed but he regretted his observations. He had intended them as a compliment but, while she was smiling, he could sense a bit of annoyance.

"I am sorry. I did not mean to pry."

She took his hand.

"Don't worry lover-boy but this is a one-night stand. You don't have to psychoanalyze me."

He smiled at her liking the feel of her hand in his.

"You are right of course,"

The reception desk at his hotel was unattended after midnight and his key was under the desk. She entered the room first and put her small bag on the dressing room table. She took a toothbrush out of it and then pulled him by the tie and kissed him gently on the lips.

"Don't take your clothes off. I like to do that," she said before disappearing into the bathroom.

He guessed this was not an unfamiliar experience for her as she seemed completely at ease. He wondered if she had ever worked as a prostitute. After being orphaned in war-time London it was probably more likely than not.

When she returned she was wearing just tan-colored bra and panties with the Tottenham scarf still wrapped round her right wrist. She looked amazing. He knew this woman must be approaching forty but she had the body of a woman half her age.

"You look incredible,"

She smiled at the compliment.

"Thank you. I like to keep fit."

She came to him; put both hands on his face and kissed him. She smelt and tasted wonderful. He felt her breasts against his chest and his penis began to harden.

She smiled as she skillfully took off his tie.

"Who wears a tie to a Football match?"

He smiled at her teasing.

"Middle-aged German businessmen do,"

She unbuttoned his shirt and then rubbed her hands over his chest and flat stomach.

"So I see you like to stay in shape yourself."

It was a bit of a lie. While he was in better shape than most men his age he was slightly overweight and his muscles lacked tone. He was a million miles away from the lethal killing machine he had once been.

"Thank you."

"That's ok. Now sit on the bed."

There was a playfulness about her now that he found captivating, although it increased his suspicion that she had been a prostitute.

She knelt on the floor and took his trousers off, smiling at his bulging underpants as she did so. She took off his shoes and socks before she smiled up at him.

"Now stand up,"

He did so and she slowly slid his underpants down his thighs.

"Y-fronts! Well aren't you Germans sexy," she said in a lilting voice.

He laughed.

"Well I wasn't planning on anyone seeing them,"

She smiled at him. He was fully erect now. She moved her head up and gently bit his inner thigh while her hair brushed his penis. After a few moments she did the same to his testicles. Karl put his hand on her head and felt his heart rate increase.

She looked up at him and then touched the base of his penis with her tongue which caused a surge of excitement through his body. She licked very slowly up to the head and then looked up at him with an impish smile.

"Please don't hurt me Sir,"

Karl's heart stopped. If the flashback earlier outside the tube-station had been sudden it was nothing to this one. It was as if a knife had slipped under his defenses and released horrific dormant memories that he had tried to bury forever.

He staggered back and she looked up at him in panic.

"What... what's wrong. I was just joking about."

He couldn't speak. He tried to regroup and follow the instructions his psychiatrist had given him. Make it like a movie so you are outside the memory looking in. So everything is happening to someone else. The girl had stood up. She looked confused and scared.

"Its...it's alright. It's not you. I...I have flashbacks."

"Ok. Try to breathe evenly. It will help you calm down."

He sat down on the bed and gradually his inner defense system kicked in. After a few minutes his breathing steadied and he looked up. Ingrid had moved back to the dressing table.

"I am sorry Ingrid. It doesn't normally happen like that, well not as bad anyway."

"Don't worry. I have bad memories too."

Karl didn't doubt it but the girl would have no idea. What could this woman, who had probably never been out of London let alone England, know of the hell of the Eastern front? He was sure losing her parents in the blitz was traumatic but he had lived for several years in a place where such a death would seem like a gift from God.

"I am sorry. It must have been scary for you."

She smiled.

"Don't worry. I think we might need to regroup though as I seem to have ruined the moment."

Karl looked down at his flaccid penis and gave a weak smile.

"Yes, sorry about that too. I am hoping it will recover," he said although, in truth, he now wanted her to leave.

She looked at him and sighed.

"Sometimes it is harder for the survivors Karl. At least the dead are free of it."

"I know what you mean. People always tell me I was one of the lucky ones and I suppose I am. Thousands of my colleagues were worked to death for many years in Siberia."

"I get that. I have been told I am lucky all my life. It is because I am the sister who survived."

"You have a sister?"

"I had loads but they are dead now."

Karl smiled sympathetically immediately feeling guilty about his earlier thoughts. So it wasn't just her Parents she had lost in the blitz.

"I am very sorry Ingrid. I suppose people mean well when they say you are lucky."

She looked sad now.

"Yes, I know they do but they don't know how my luck manifested itself."

He looked down at his lifeless penis again. He needed her to go. The flashbacks always left him depressed and her sad story was not helping matters. It was a shame because he had liked her.

"I think we need to call it a night Ingrid. I am sorry but I am a bit messed up right now. "

"You are probably right."

He felt awkward, as if he had snubbed her. He smiled weakly.

"Thank you for being so understanding. How did you get to be lucky?"

"Do you really want to know?"

Karl didn't. He wanted her to go but she deserved politeness.

"Yes I do."

He looked down and gathered his clothes before she replied; hoping to hurry her out.

"I was lucky because I was being raped somewhere else when my sisters died."

He stared at her. He did the maths in his head. It was during the blitz. She couldn't have been more than 10-years-old.

"Oh my God Ingrid, that is horrible; you poor thing. Who was it, an Uncle or something?"

"No he wasn't an Uncle. He called himself a soldier but he was not worthy of the name. He was just an evil cunt."

The use of the word shocked him. It was an ugly word and seemed obscene on her lips. He pulled on his underpants and trousers and then sat down to put his shoes on. He was desperate for her to leave now but she was showing no sign of dressing. He looked up.

"So what happened? Did the bomb miss the room you were in?"

She looked at him for several seconds; a blank look on her face. She picked up her bag which Karl hoped was a sign she was about to go to the bathroom and get dressed.

"My sisters did not die in the blitz."

He looked at her in surprise.

"Oh sorry I misunderstood. How did they die?"

She gave him a pensive look as if deciding whether to tell him.

"I can't say for certain about all of them although I can be pretty sure. But I do know how Karolina, Ruth and Sarah died."

She looked calm. She stood with her bottom resting on the table, still in just panties and bra and with the Tottenham scarf round her right wrist.

"If this is making you uncomfortable Ingrid you don't have to tell me. It is none of my business and I, more than anyone, know about painful memories."

"No that's alright."

She said nothing more. She just kept looking at him or rather through him.

"So," he said quietly. "How did they die?"

She looked away for a few seconds before looking back at him. Her face was blank and devoid of emotion as she spoke.

"You shot them in the head Karl."

Chapter Three

It took her over a second to pull the gun from the bag. It was true she took her time but once it would have been enough. In his prime Karl could have been across the room and breaking her neck in the blink of an eye.

But he was a long way from his prime.

He remembered that first day at the training camp. "Can a trained German soldier ever be caught by surprise?" had shouted the instructor.

"No" had been the bellowed reply of the hundred trainees.

"Wrong answer. Anyone can be caught by surprise. It is not a crime. But a German soldier will be able to recover from that surprise quicker than anyone alive."

And once he would have. Once his first reaction would not have been to ask himself how the danger had come, it would have been to neutralize that danger.

But not now, now he looked at the woman; his mouth open in shock. He had been completely blind-sided. For a second he even wondered if he was dreaming.

"I… I don't understand,"

"I will give you some time. Maybe you will have another of your flashbacks."

He stared at her for over a minute trying to recover from the shock. He saw that the pistol had a silencer.

"Ingrid. I did not kill your sisters. As I said before I was not in the Luftwaffe and I have never met you before."

"I know what you were in Karl. It is called the Waffen SS. I also know you were a guard at Belsen concentration camp in 1945 and for two years before that."

Karl was still having problems believing what was happening but his training was coming back to him. He had to stall and look for his chance.

"None of that is true Ingrid. I served in the regular army in Russia. I served in Poland too but not in the camps."

Still keeping the gun on him she unwrapped the scarf from her wrist then turned it towards him. Karl saw the tattoo that was her camp number immediately. She said nothing.

"Your English is perfect. Where are you from?"

"Holland,"

"Ingrid I am sorry for what happened to you and I am sorry about the Holocaust but I was not there. I don't know how you identified me but you have the wrong man."

She was very still. Karl was alert now, looking for an opportunity but she didn't look stressed about holding a gun on him. She looked trained. The unusually fit body and the intelligence she couldn't quite hide should have told him that.

"I thought you would say that Karl."

Without moving the gun a millimeter she reached into her bag with her other hand, took out a yellow envelope and tossed it to him.

"Open it and read it."

Now he had it in his hands he saw that the envelope had in fact once been white. But it was yellowed with age. He opened it and took out a single sheet of paper.

"This is the German translation. I have another in English."

It was dated the 25th of April 1945, ten days after the liberation of Belsen. At the top of the page was the name Karl Muller. Under it were the words "Identification marks"

He stared at the list feeling his panic rise as he saw the list of scars and birth-marks on his body. The scarred index finger was there from when he had burnt it as a child. The scar on his right elbow and the one on his neck from the motor-cycle accident were there. They also described his dental fillings.

Everything was documented including his unusual belly button, the shape of his nipples and the exact position of his SS blood group tattoo. Even the size of his erect penis was estimated.

He kept staring at it long after he had finished reading. He thought of his wife. He thought of his son who was about to be married. Ingrid did not say a word.

"Are you Mossad?" he said without looking up.

"Do you still think I have got the wrong person Karl?"

The fact she didn't answer his question suggested she had at least been trained by the Israeli secret service. It was a far from comforting thought.

"Where did you get this?"

"It was dictated to a British officer. The British never found you. I think in the beginning they tried hard but you were good at hiding your tracks and they had bigger fish to fry. But I never stopped looking Karl."

"I.... I don't understand."

"What don't you understand Karl? How I found you or how I survived?"

"Both,"

He had to keep her talking. It was his only chance. She was making a mistake. She should have killed him before now. It was unprofessional. But she couldn't. It would be unsatisfactory. She had hunted him for thirty years. She needed to draw it out; boast about how she had found him.

"Felix wanted another go. You had shot 3 of my sisters then you told Felix to take one of the others into the other room and kill her. You told him to hurry as the Captain was on his way and, as all sexual contact with the dirty Jews was strictly forbidden, you had to destroy the evidence. But Felix couldn't resist another session with a 10-year-old cunt so he disobeyed you. After he finished she scrambled away and hid in the latrine."

Felix Ritter. Karl remembered him. Spotty Ritter they had called him because of his terrible acne. They also called him virgin Ritter and he almost certainly had been until that day.

"Do you remember it Karl? Do you remember how you and 5 men under your command raped six sisters, the oldest being 16 and the youngest 7. Do you remember shooting them in the head afterwards Karl? Do you remember after you had raped 7-year-old Eva you laughed and told the others that she had the tightest cunt? I can understand if you don't remember Karl because I am sure they weren't the first children you raped and murdered."

Karl couldn't speak. He felt sick.

"Do you remember Karl?"

It was a full minute before he replied.

"I wish I didn't,"

She didn't speak and he kept looking at the floor. Eventually he looked up at her. He had no recollection of her as a child. But he knew she spoke the truth.

"I am sorry Ingrid. I was a different person then. I was a monster."

"Now we get to the bit where you were brain-washed as a child, how you were conditioned to hate the Jews from a young age, how you were only following orders. Please tell me you were a victim too Karl. I love that one."

It was what he was going to say but he knew how pathetic it sounded even without her mockery.

"None of it is untrue Ingrid but of course I am not a victim like you were. But I am a changed man. I know the truth now. I know what Hitler and the Nazi's really were. I hate them for what they turned me into."

"And when did this revelation come to pass Karl. When did you stop being an SS Nazi?"

"It was 1960 and it was here in England. I saw that Hitler had been evil and had made me evil. I remembered what I had done to you and many others. I cried Ingrid. I give money to Jewish charities now and pray for the victims of the Holocaust."

"Do you know how I found you Karl?"

He looked at her. He had to try to survive. In a way he wanted to die and he knew he deserved to. But he had a wife and a son who was about to be married. He had to keep her talking. He also wanted to know.

"No, I don't,"

"It took a long time and you were very clever. You were a Sergeant when I knew you but before Belsen was liberated you were smart enough to get yourself demoted to a private soldier and transferred. You knew the lower the rank the less effort the allies would put into finding you. Also the further down the chain of command the more valid the "I was only following orders" plea."

Karl was shocked, as it was all true, but he had the beginnings of a plan in mind. He had survived the allies and he would survive this.

"Then of course there was the name change. You were clever here too. After the war the allies didn't allow ex-soldiers to change their names but you had done it long before. You used the name Muller at the camp but you had officially changed it to your step-fathers name soon after being posted to Belsen. For a fanatical SS man you seem to have taken a lot of precautions just in case you really weren't the master race."

There would be a moment. He had to keep his eyes locked on hers.

"So the British couldn't trace you and neither could I. Guards and inmates spoke of a Sergeant Muller but there was no written record of such a man serving at Belsen."

He would wait for a loud noise from either the hall-way or the street: maybe an exhaust misfire. She would look to the window and he would pounce. And even if there wasn't a noise he still thought he could distract her.

"So what was I to do? Where was I to start? I didn't even know what part of Germany you came from. So I travelled to every part and, because your voice had been in my head for nearly 30 years, I recognized the Bavarian accent when I heard it."

He couldn't rely on a noise. He had to keep his eyes on hers. Then suddenly he would glance at the window. In his training he had been told very few people, however well trained, could resist human instinct. If he could keep his eyes locked on hers they would follow his when he looked to the window.

"But of course Bavaria was big with a large population. I had significantly reduced the size of the haystack but it was still a haystack."

When her eyes went to the window his initial movement had to be slightly to his left. Her arm would move to her right as she looked but when she panicked she would bring it back too fast and too far. If he got it right the bullet would miss him to his right. And then he would be on her.

"I seemed to have hit a dead-end but then I had an idea. I went to Munich on the 9th of November."

He looked at her feeling stunned and slightly sick. She was good. She was very good.

"Yes Karl, the 9th of November when pathetic old Nazi's congregate in Munich to celebrate Hitler's doomed beer-hall Putsch. Now, of course the authorities don't let you march anymore but it wasn't hard to find out where the secret gathering was."

She was right. They had been pathetic. A bunch of old men, along with a few young skin-head neo-Nazi's, drinking themselves stupid and deluding themselves that they would rise again.

"I sat in a café opposite Karl. I sat there a long time but then there you were. You were older but I recognized you instantly. I watched you walk into the bar and after about 10 minutes I followed you in. You weren't there obviously but I saw the neo-Nazi's guarding the back-room. Do you know when this was Karl?"

"You don't understand..."

"It was 1969 Karl. Just three years ago. 9 years after your supposed conversion. 9 years after you realized how evil Hitler had been. Can you explain that to me Karl?"

"I have to go. You have to understand. We all have to go. The SS zealots are always on the look-out for anyone they consider has betrayed the oath. I have to attend this and Hitler's birthday. If I miss both in a year I and my family would be in danger. You have to believe me."

She didn't speak for nearly a minute.

"I do believe you Karl."

He looked at her. Maybe there was still hope. Maybe she hadn't come to kill him.

"I watched you, on and off, for 2 years to see if you could lead me to the others. And then I had an idea. If the old SS gather for the beer-hall putsch then maybe individual units gather as well on significant dates. Maybe your old unit gathers on the anniversary of the liberation of Belsen. It was a long-shot but a year ago I decided to follow you for a week before the date."

He stayed silent hardly daring to hope.

"And you did go to Belsen but not to meet your old comrades. I have to say I was shocked to see you lay a wreath at the memorial and to sign the book of remembrance. I was just two places behind you when you put what looked like a considerable amount of money into the charity box."

"I have been many times. I am truly sorry for my actions during the war Ingrid. I am ashamed of them."

"That action saved your life. It threw me off balance. It challenged my certainty that what I was planning was right."

She paused while looking at Karl with a blank face. He kept his face passive but in his mind he made a decision.

"It was hard, even painful, to admit that you clearly did regret what you had done."

"I really do,"

"But do you know what Karl?"

Karl kept his eyes locked on hers.

"Yes. I know. It is not enough. But I can do no more. I can't bring your sisters back Ingrid."

"You see Karl I promised them. I promised them I would survive and that one day I would kill you all."

For a few glorious seconds, after she talked of his visit to Belsen, Karl had allowed himself to believe she would let him live. But then reality had intruded. He had raped her and her sisters. Then he had murdered her siblings. No matter how much he regretted that fact, and how much she believed he had changed, only one of them was leaving this room alive.

"My son knows you came back with me. He will find me here. He knows your friends in the pub. The police will find you. You can't get away with it Ingrid."

"They don't know my real name Karl. I met them only six months ago just after I learnt you were coming here for this match. They kno..."

Karl glanced sharply to the window and exploded off the bed, his body twisting to his left. It had to be now when she was talking and just before she killed him. It was the moment when she was most vulnerable. Her brain had two things to concentrate on; her words of explanation and the imminent murder of a man in cold blood. His glance to the window would add a third and that should be too much.

As the manual said; very few people, however well-trained, can resist human instinct.

The first bullet hit him in the right side of his chest.

He had got maybe half a meter off the bed and, because he had moved to his left, the impact flipped him onto his back as he landed on the floor.

He felt remarkably little pain and he knew his body had gone into shock. He tried to move but his limbs seemed disconnected. He saw her move to stand over him. She looked down at him with the gun aimed at his head. She didn't look unkind. If anything she looked sad.

He tried to speak; to beg for mercy.

Without changing her expression she pulled the trigger.

Chapter Four

Sophie switched the lights on and off three times; her signal for Joe. She took Karl's wallet and his wrist-watch. Then she quickly dressed. From her bag she took plastic gloves and some anti-septic wipes. She wiped the gun clean before putting it into the bag. Then she wiped down every hard surface she had touched.

She listened at the door before poking her head out into the hall. She looked down at Karl for a second then quickly left. She walked slowly; just another woman leaving a hotel room in the middle of the night after illicit sex. She met no one.

When she came out of the hotel she turned left and continued walking, inwardly cursing her limp. Joe's Ford Escort passed her and turned right about half-a-mile down the street. She turned left until she hit a busy road which she crossed. She did three more crossings before she come to the train station. She entered and found the toilets.

She saw one of the five cubicles was occupied. She took the one at the end. Once inside she took off the wig to reveal short black hair. Then she peeled off the stick-on birth-mark. Lastly she turned the Tottenham football shirt inside out to reveal a plain blue shirt.

She heard the toilet flush in the occupied cubicle and waited for the occupant to leave. Once she had done so Sophie also left. She went into the station and walked to the exit pleased with the fact she no longer had to limp. She found the Ford a street away and quickly got into the passenger seat. Joe moved off immediately without a word.

It was probably five minutes before he spoke.

"Is he dead?"

"Yes, very"

"He made me kill Ruud,"

She knew the story well.

"He was my best friend. He made us fight to the death with shovels while he and his friends laughed. He made me kill my best friend. We were both twelve."

"Well he is dead now Joe,"

He paused, his face grim.

"I wish I had been there."

"I know but we have to stick to the plan Joe."

"Yes. I know I am just the back-up."

Sophie was tired of this but kept her voice calm. They were his sisters too.

"It is important Joe. I need you there. I could never do it without you. But we both know I am better suited to the confrontation. I can hide the hatred and you can't."

Joe didn't answer and Sophie didn't want to talk. She knew what was coming and knew this time, because it was personal, it would be different and almost certainly worse.

It was called the aftermath and the psychologists had told her it couldn't be ignored. She had to get away, find some silent space and deal with the implications of killing a man. At the moment she still had to be alert but once she felt safe she would relax and it would start. And, despite his frustration and bitterness, Joe knew he couldn't trouble her unduly now.

The psychologists had told them both that Joe should not be in at the kill. They had been understanding of his frustration but also brutally honest. They had both been damaged by their childhood experiences but Sophie could put her emotions aside and be cold and efficient and Joe couldn't.

Privately Sol, her main mentor, had told her she shouldn't take Joe with her at all.

"He is a liability Sophie."

"You think the hatred will show. I know that. I will only use him for support."

"It's not just the hatred Sophie. The main problem is the fear."

"He is not a coward Sol. He has never shown cowardice."

"No I know. He is fit, very strong and, in normal circumstances, as brave as a lion. But the brain is a funny thing. Joe was rightly petrified of these men for 2 of his childhood years and those memories are still in his head. When he comes face to face with them again those memories will resurface and he is likely to react as he did as a child. It won't matter that he is now much stronger than them. He is liable to panic. This is not conjecture Sophie. We have seen it happen. It is why we don't encourage agents having personal connections to targets."

"But I was just as petrified. So you don't think I will panic?"

"It is different for you although, as I have said many times, I would prefer you to go after targets we choose. But you have processed your trauma in a different way to Joe."

It wasn't a compliment. What Sol had meant was that she was a little more emotionally dead than Joe was.

She pulled the handle to recline the seat a little more and laid back. She tried not to think of Karl but the memories of their flirting in the pub and the comfortable walk to his hotel kept coming back to her. She didn't regret his death, and no one could say he didn't deserve it, but there was no doubt that, whatever he had once been, she had murdered a decent man.

"I will miss them Sophie. They were good lads."

"I know Joe. It was a good time."

It was true. She had learnt of Karl's plans to come to the match over seven months before and she had then come to London to prepare. She and Joe had integrated themselves with the group of Tottenham fans six months before and she had come to enjoy their company.

They drank too much and could sometimes be violent to rival fans but, for one of the few times in her life, she felt part of something. She had hardly known the rules of football but she began to enjoy the tribal element to it.

But she had never lost sight of the fact she was building a false persona.

"Did he beg?"

"No, not really,"

"Did he remember you?"

"No,"

"Did you tell him what he had done to you?"

"Yes,"

"Did you tell him what he had done to me?"

"Yes, I did Joe,"

"Was he sorry?"

"We already knew he was sorry Joe,"

"Was it hard, to kill him I mean?"

"No,"

"What did you think about as you did it?"

This time the lie didn't come so easily. How could she tell him that all she could think about was that Karl would not be at his son's wedding.

"I thought of him shooting Karolina in the head."

Chapter Five

"So, what have we got Dan?"

Detective Sergeant Dan Coates turned to see his boss Detective Chief Inspector Ron Bennett enter the room.

"A very dead German by the name of Karl Bauman. He was 53-years-old and over for the Tottenham Bayern match last night. He has been shot, once in the chest and once in the head. His wallet and wrist-watch are missing. The prime suspect is a woman, about 37, called Ingrid."

"Who found the body?"

"His son who was in the next room. They were meant to be checking out at 9 this morning. When he didn't show the son got the maid to open the door. He is being comforted next door."

"So what do we know about this Ingrid?"

"The German boys met a group of Tottenham fans before the match. Afterwards they met up in The Coach and Horses on Seven Sisters road. The victim left with the woman at about midnight. We have a decent description from the Germans but I hope to get a better one when I trace the Tottenham fans."

"So are we working on the theory that they came back for sex and then this Ingrid decided to rob him, the victim resisted and she shot him?"

"That is how it looks."

"You sound a little dubious. Is there anything that contradicts that?"

"There are a couple of things the first being that she had a gun, with a silencer, with her at all. They are hard to get and does this woman really carry one to a football match?"

"Good point, anything else?"

"Yes. The Germans describe this girl as a bit of a loud-mouthed drinker but she was clearly very efficient with the weapon. It looks almost like an execution; one in the chest to put him down and one in the brain to finish him off."

"Is there any reason someone would want to execute him?"

Dan looked him in the eye.

"Yes, possibly there is."

He moved to the body.

"We can't move him yet but look at the inside of his upper arm.

Ron saw the blood-group tattoo immediately and Dan saw him shudder. He stared at it for nearly a minute.

"Well, well, well, we have a member of the SS amongst us. So what are you thinking Dan?"

"Well if Ingrid was from around here there is a possibility she was Jewish."

Ron thought about it.

"It is a possibility. She sees the tattoo and decides to kill him. But it is unlikely. I don't want the tattoo to sidetrack us. The most likely scenario is the robbery gone wrong one. We also may have to consider that she was on the game and the man didn't want to pay. It is not that strange for whores to be armed for protection although the silencer is highly unusual. Find out more about the woman and keep an open mind."

Dan spent the morning talking to the couple who ran the pub and six of the Tottenham fans. It was late afternoon when he reported back to Ron.

"Her and her elder brother appeared about six months ago. According to her mates she was a secretary but none of them knew where. She supposedly shared a flat with her brother in Neasden although no one had actually visited her there. She seems a bit of a tart to be honest. She had casual sex with at least three of the fans. The landlady of the pub suspected she was on the game as she always seemed to have plenty of money and she had seen her disappearing with older men."

"Did any of the guys back that up?"

"None of them knew for certain but most thought it likely that she at least dabbled in prostitution."

"Was she Jewish?"

"No one knew for certain but most thought it doubtful. She never talked about religion."

"Any family?"

"According to the guys her parents were killed in the Blitz which I suppose opens up the revenge idea again."

"What else did they say about her?"

"They all liked her. They reckon she was a bit distant and withdrawn at first but she opened up later. They thought she had had some bad experiences but she really seemed to enjoy the drinking and the football."

"Did you tell them about the murder?"

"Yes and they were pretty shocked. They knew she had gone out with the German and they suspect she probably wanted paying and he refused."

"Did any of them suggest the meeting with the Germans was anything but accidental?"

"No. They just come out of the tube station at the same time."

"But was she behind the timetable? Did she suggest what time they gathered and got the tube?"

"I asked that but none of them recall her being the instigator. It doesn't look pre-planned."

"No it doesn't but that doesn't mean it wasn't."

"From the interviews she didn't seem that intelligent or manipulative."

"A Mossad agent would like to give a false impression."

"Do you really think she is Mossad?"

Ron thought about it.

"No not really. I think it more likely she is a whore who didn't get paid. But we know that Mossad has carried out a lot of these operations across Europe so we can't dismiss it."

"They haven't done much in England as far as I know. If they targeted Bauman wouldn't they have killed him in Germany?"

"Yes, that's why it's unlikely. Also, while they would have laid a false trail they wouldn't have spent six months doing it. "

"If she is as she appears to be she shouldn't be hard to catch."

"No she shouldn't. I saw the description; a permanent limp and a very visual birth-mark on her face. It should be a piece of piss to find her. But there are certain anomalies about the cheated whore scenario. Did you get anything else?"

"There may be something. They said the girl had an East-End of London accent but the brother, Joe, occasionally had what one of the guys called a foreign inflection. Apparently he spent a lot of the last 10 years working in Holland and picked up the accent."

"Why do you think that might be significant?"

"This is pure speculation but what if Ingrid was originally Dutch? What if she had been a Dutch Jew? She might have been a Holocaust survivor who came to English relatives as a child after the war. What would have been her reaction to the tattoo if that had been the case?"

Ron was silent.

"Well I know if I had a gun in my bag I would have shot the bastard. Keep it in mind Dan, and get Bauman's war record, but we have no evidence for that. Concentrate on what we know for now. Get the description to every force in London and give it to the press. If everything is as it seems she should be in custody by close of play tomorrow."

But she wasn't.

Chapter Six

Kurt Hoffman watched his boss leave the hotel and then drove his Mercedes to the door. The concierge waved at him angrily but Kurt ignored him; he hated the English. Dieter Braun, the assistant head of the German trade delegation, got in the back and Kurt edged into the busy traffic.

"Where to boss?"

"The Retreat. I have a birthday present for you."

Kurt looked back at his smiling boss.

"Really, what kind of present?"

"One I think you are really going to like. Robert phoned me and told me he had found a special that is going to be right up your street."

Kurt felt his excitement grow.

"How old?"

"I am told she is about 38,"

"I am not being funny boss but that is way too old for my tastes. Actually it is about 30 years too old."

Braun laughed.

"Trust me Kurt. When have I ever let you down?"

Kurt smiled as the answer was never. He loved his job as his principal boss had similar tastes to him. And in him, Kurt was also aware, that Braun had found the perfect employee.

Dieter Braun had made a fortune in the construction industry in post-war Germany. With the Allies pouring money into the rebuilding of the wrecked cities, as Germany became the front-line in the cold war, there was huge money to be made by an ambitious man.

But Dieter Braun was not only ambitious. He was also completely ruthless and that's where Kurt came in. For Braun, the very strong, completely amoral, absolutely loyal former SS man, was ideal.

Officially he was his chauffeur/bodyguard but in reality he was his enforcer. Rivals for contracts would be intimidated, beaten up and, if this wasn't enough, disappeared. Any journalist who dared write anything negative about Braun would receive a late night visit from Kurt; a visit that would leave them terrified, physically injured or dead.

For Braun it was an ideal arrangement. For Kurt it was like the good old days.

It took them 30 minutes to drive to the house in Earls Court. Braun smiled at him as they got out of the car.

"Try to control your excitement Kurt. You can have your fun but I have promised Robert no dead bodies to deal with."

"Ok boss, where did he find her?"

"She came to him looking for a job; she was pretty desperate by all accounts. Robert didn't want her as she was too old for most of his punters but then he saw something that made him think of you."

"No, he saw something that made him think about how much you would pay him."

Braun laughed.

"Yes and it is quite a lot. But you deserve it on your birthday."

"I can't imagine why he would think I would want an old woman though."

"You will see,"

They rang the bell and Robert let them in. He was a middle-aged hard looking man with a prominent gold tooth.

"Hi Dieter. You have explained the rules to Kurt haven't you?"

"Yes I have and he has promised to behave reasonably well."

"Yes, well just in case I have sent the girls home apart from her and Lucy, who I know is your favorite Dieter."

They went into the lounge and Robert poured them both a brandy. Then he went down the hall to knock on one of the bedroom doors.

"Ok Lucy, you can bring her out now."

Lucy appeared first. She was a tall blonde of about 25 dressed in stockings and suspenders with a flimsy negligee covering her breasts. Normally she was always smiling but today she looked pensive. Kurt guessed that she would know what was coming for the new girl.

If she looked pensive the woman behind her looked terrified. Kurt thought Dieter had been winding him up about her age because, at first glance, she looked like a child. But then he realized she wasn't as small as she first appeared. She was just shrunken with fear.

Kurt felt his cock harden slightly. Is this what Dieter had meant. He knew he liked them very young but he also liked them to be terrified. It wasn't perfect, and Kurt was a bit disappointed in his boss, but it would do.

She was dressed in just creamed colored cotton bra and panties with flowers on. Kurt wondered if Robert had chosen these to make her look younger. She had badly cut jet black hair. She looked slim rather than skinny but her face looked unhealthily pale. She wasn't unattractive but she was far from young.

"Is she English?" he asked.

"No," said Robert. "She is originally from Poland. She doesn't speak very much English but I gather she was smuggled back to England by a British army officer at the end of the war. He was married but kept her in a flat somewhere as his whore. He died last year and the officer's son kicked her out on her arse. She knows no one in England, has no money, so ended up here."

Kurt looked at her. From her expression it was clear she had understood very little of what was said. He walked towards her. She was trembling with fear and this was causing his cock to harden even more. Ever since the camps he had loved people to be scared of him; to know that he had the power of life and death over them.

He touched her cheek and she shuddered.

"She looks like she will be fun boss but I still don't see why she is ideal for me."

"Look at her arm Kurt,"

He saw it immediately. It was so familiar. For a time it had been his job to mark them with the blue tattoo that was their camp number. He stared at it.

"Oh my God boss, I fucking love you. This is the best present ever."

Braun laughed.

"I still want you to remember your promise Kurt."

That would be a hard promise to keep but Kurt knew he had to. The fall-out from dead bodies could be managed in Germany and the deaths were planned weeks in advance.

Random killings in a foreign country were a different matter and could bring scandal to the name Dieter Braun.

But it really wasn't fair in this case. The girl knew no one in England and no authority would have a record of her. It was as if she never existed. He could easily kill her without consequences.

And Kurt so wanted to kill her. He felt the old anger growing as he stared at the trembling girl. She had seen him look at the number and seen his reaction. She now seemed almost paralyzed with fear.

He stared at the woman and then pushed her to the hall.

"Get in the bedroom bitch."

The woman looked at both Dieter and Robert but they just stared back at her with blank faces. Lucy looked away. Then, seemingly resigned to her fate, the woman walked through the bedroom door. Kurt looked at Dieter.

"I will keep my promise boss but she will pay for what those Jews did. Some very good SS men were hung because of bitches like her. They lined up in court to tell their lies. Some good friends of mine spent years in prison. I bet when that bitch was whoring herself out to that British officer she was laughing at us. I have dreamed of a day like this."

Dieter smiled.

"Well have fun and while you do the lovely Lucy will be entertaining me in the other room."

Kurt nodded and walked into the bedroom closing the door behind him. The girl was standing by the bed trembling. He stood just in front of her. She looked tiny compared to him; tiny and pathetic.

"Look at me bitch,"

She slowly looked up at him. The terror in her eyes brought back so many memories.

"I bet you thought you had escaped didn't you? I bet when you were living it up in London with the officer you thought you had escaped the SS."

He pushed her roughly in the chest and she fell back onto the bed.

"Well think again bitch because the SS never give up. One day we will rise again and wipe you Jewish scum off the face of the Earth."

As she lay there; passive and terrified, he quickly stripped. His cock was rock-hard. He looked at her and then jumped on the bed. His knees landed astride her legs and he had intended to grab her shoulders. But it never happened.

As he landed her arm shot out straight; her fingers smashing into his throat. The combination of her driven arm and his momentum was devastating. He screamed as he fell off the bed but hardly a sound come out of his mouth.

He sprawled on the floor in shock and agony. But the girl was moving and moving incredibly quickly. He looked up at her just as she drove her elbow into his face. He felt his nose break instantly.

He fell back; his panic building. He put one hand on the floor to push himself up but she grabbed the arm and threw her body over his back. Kurt felt his shoulder joint dislocate and experienced the worst pain of his life.

He screamed for help but again there was little sound and his throat was in agony. With a sense of horror he realized that she may have permanently destroyed his voice box.

She had left him now but the slightest movement was causing him incredible agony. He turned his body so he was on the floor with his back resting against the bed. He was in complete shock.

She looked down at him. For a second he had hoped she would run. He had hoped she, in her panic, had just got lucky. But one look at her calm face told him this was not the case.

"Who... who are you?"

Every word was agony and even then they just come out as a whisper. She ignored him and then picked up her bag. Kurt watched her pull out the gun with the silencer.

"Please...please don't kill me,"

She pointed the gun at him, her face calm and impassive. Kurt felt his bowels release.

"I was at Belsen concentration camp in 1945. I was 10-years-old. You and your colleagues raped and murdered 6 sisters. Do you remember the incident?"

Kurt did. There had been many such incidents but they had thought the six sisters thing was amusing.

"No... No. It wasn't me."

His voice was little more than a whisper but he could hear the panic in it.

The woman looked at him.

"Yes it was,"

Then she shot him twice; once in the heart and once in the head.

Chapter Seven

Sophie quickly dressed then, holding the gun, left the room. She found Robert in the lounge, glass in hand, watching TV. He looked up at her. His face registered shock and then he froze when he saw the gun pointed at him.

"Kneel on the floor."

He did so while looking terrified.

"Who are you?"

Sophie kept the gun on him while she looked him in the eye.

"If you give the police a good description of me we will come back and kill you. Dispose of the body secretly if you can but if you can't make up some bull-shit about me. Tell Lucy and the Kraut that too. And if you or he tries to find me we will kill you. Now lie on the floor and stay there for ten minutes after I have left."

He did so. Sophie hesitated for a second; fighting the urge to shoot Robert and the German. But, no, she had to stick to the plan.

She quickly left. Earls Court underground station was two minutes away. She had bought several tickets earlier and jumped on the first train available. She changed several times until she arrived at Kings Cross where she got off.

She met Joe at the hotel room he had booked earlier where she changed clothes and removed the black wig and the whitening lotion on her face.

"I still think we should have killed them. It is not as if they didn't deserve it" said Joe.

"We can't kill every bad person Joe. Besides, there were practical reasons not to."

"Dieter Braun may come after you. He is a rich man."

"I doubt it. Hoffman was just an employee at the end of the day. Braun will think we are Mossad and he won't want to mess with them. He will be gone from there long before any police arrive. He won't want his name associated with dead SS men at a London brothel. But if I had killed him it would have caused a shit-storm in the media and we would have every police force in Europe after us."

Joe said nothing more on the matter and ten minutes later they were on the Piccadilly line heading towards Heathrow airport.

Chapter Eight

Dan found Ron in his office. He was on the phone and waved Dan into a chair. He finished the phone call and looked at him expectantly.

"I think we need to rethink the Bauman case," said Dan.

"As she would have stood out like a sore thumb and we have had not a single report about her I suspect you are right."

"I think she was in disguise the whole six months she was drinking with the other Tottenham fans. I think the birth-mark, the hair, and possibly the limp, were fake."

"If that is the case it has big implications Dan."

"I know but there are two other things. Bauman was a concentration camp guard at Belsen. And I interviewed the fans again. In 6 months none of them saw her right wrist. She always had either a Spurs scarf round it or a bandage. She even had the scarf on when she had sex."

"So you think she was hiding her camp number?"

"I think that has to be a strong possibility."

"Where did you find out about Bauman's service record?"

"I contacted the German embassy and they put me in touch with the Munich police."

"Well contact them again and find out if a Kurt Hoffman was also a camp guard. You can ask if he ever served with Bauman."

"Who is Kurt Hoffman?"

"He is a German, with an SS tattoo, who was yesterday shot dead in a brothel in Earls Court."

"Jesus Christ,"

Ron smiled.

"No, it was a woman,"

"How many witnesses?"

"Two, a pimp and one prostitute. The pimp called the police but forensics think the time of death was earlier than they claimed. The chaps on the scene think there was someone else there who they are protecting. The descriptions were contradictory to say the least but I think we can assume it was our Ingrid. If we can connect Bauman and Hoffman I think that would probably confirm it."

"What was her story this time?"

Ron told him the story about the Holocaust survivor from Poland.

"It seems she turned up desperate for work and the pimp knew Hoffman would shoot his load with excitement at, fucking, and probably beating the shit out of, a Jewish camp survivor."

"Christ, the pimp seems a piece of work. Do you think there is any truth in the girl's story?"

"It is possible but I doubt it very much. If we link both cases it would seem it was just a story Ingrid told to get into a room alone with Hoffman. I think we might be dealing with someone who is very clever and very motivated."

"Do you think there is a Mossad connection?"

"I think we have to assume she is Mossad trained but the six months planning for Bauman suggests to me that she is working independently."

"So that would mean she had personal experience of Bauman and Hoffman; that she was at Belsen."

Ron looked at him.

"I know what you are thinking Dan because I am thinking it too. But we are policemen. It doesn't matter how justified the killer is, we are duty bound to try to catch her."

"Yes I understand that Ron."

"You need to because one day you may come face to face with her and you have to remember that she is a killer. Any hesitation on your part could mean you are dead."

"Do we know anything about the client at the brothel who disappeared?"

"We think it was maybe Dieter Braun. He was Hoffman's boss. He is a very rich guy with a questionable reputation. I doubt we will get anything from him as he will deny he was there. We need to find a link between Hoffman and Bauman."

"If they were both at Belsen at the same time surely that would be a link."

"It would be yes but there is a guy I want you to see even if they weren't. His name is Colonel Radcliffe. He is a long-time retired but in 1945 he was a Captain who interviewed hundreds of Belsen survivors for the war crimes committees. I was on the phone to him when you came in. He kept extensive records and copies. I said you would meet him tomorrow. He lives in a village near Watford."

"That shouldn't be a problem. Was there anything else?"

Ron looked at him.

"Yes. He also says not to eat before you come as you are likely to bring it back up."

Chapter Nine

Colonel Radcliffe was in his late sixties and, like most retired army officers, immaculately turned out in a tweed suit with a brown tie. He introduced Dan to his wife before he led him to the large patio where there was a table, two chairs and 3 wooden crates.

"In these boxes are the testimonies of 785 Belsen survivors. I have to warn you that they make for harrowing reading. There are normally two pages. One is what the survivors claim was done to them or crimes that they witnessed. The second page is hopefully the name of the guard and identifying marks."

"I am sorry Sir but how do you come to have these. Surely the authorities or the courts should have them."

"Don't worry Sergeant. They did, and maybe still do have copies. But the war crimes commissions were closed down twenty-four years ago and I suspect their copies were destroyed. The Army gave their copies to the German police but, if they survive at all, they are buried in a vault. I made a third copy for myself."

"Why did you do that?"

"Because they are important documents Sergeant and should not be destroyed to suit modern political sensitivities. Even now, just twenty-seven years later, some people deny the Holocaust happened. It seems a ludicrous claim right now as there are so many survivors still alive. But when they are all dead in 50 years or so can you imagine how persuasive that claim will be?"

"I take your point. I have already heard people say that it is just Israel spreading lies."

"Anyone who visited Belsen in 1945 would never make such a claim and in the east it was even worse."

Dan looked down at the boxes daunted by the task ahead.

"When did you last read them?"

"Until your DCI rang I hadn't looked at them in years. But I glanced over them last night to see if I could find any references to Bauman and Hoffman."

"And did you?"

"I found a lot of references to Hoffman but none to Bauman."

"But we know Bauman was there."

"Yes. Corporal Bauman came to Belsen in November 1943 and was promoted to Sergeant soon after. He was demoted to private just before Belsen was liberated. All this is on his official record."

"But none of the survivors make claims about him. Does that make him decent or something? Are there any other guards who were there who were not accused?"

"There were a few who did not feature but none who had been there as long as Bauman. It could be a possible reason for his demotion; that he was not cruel enough. But I doubt it. It is probably more to do with him wanting the lowest rank possible if captured by the allies as this would possibly make him less culpable. You have to understand that the SS soldiers, especially the camp guards, were conditioned to be unsympathetic and brutal, to the Jews especially. Anything less was seen as weakness and punished."

"So how do you explain why no one makes a claim against Bauman?"

"At the moment I can't explain it. It could be as simple as the victims never knew his name."

"But he had been there for quite a long time."

"That is true, and it is unlikely, but very often the victims didn't live long enough to learn the names."

Dan thought about that. This was not going to be pleasant.

"I will try to rustle up some tea while you make a start."

Dan watched him walk away and then looked at the boxes. They were labeled by the years 1942 to 1945. There were very few folders in the first box and hundreds in the last. He decided to work backwards and picked up the first folder in the 1945 box.

"Testimony of Klara Schippers aged 44"
Interviewer
Captain Jeffrey Radcliffe
Translator
Paul Van Rooyen
Date of interview 27/4/1945
Interviewer's notes
Although still traumatized and very underweight the subject, a Dutch national, is of sound mind and lucid.

"On the 1st day of the New Year some of the off-duty guards were clearly drunk. Six men under the command of Sergeant Muller emptied our barracks and made us strip and stand to attention outside. The temperature was well below freezing. They picked two women, gave them wooden clubs, and made them fight naked in the snow. One woman was

Polish but I didn't know her name. The other lady was called Femke and she was from Amsterdam.

The guards took bets on who would win and the women were told that the loser, if she was still alive, would be hung up and hosed down with cold water for 10 minutes.

The Polish woman had been transported from the east and was very weak. Soon she was barely conscious and was declared the loser. They hung her up and laughed as they soaked her. She froze to death. Then they chose two more one of which was me.

I had to fight a very weak lady who was nearly sixty. She was a kind woman who I had seen giving a part of her ration to a sick child two days earlier; this despite being on the verge of starvation herself. I caved her skull in with the club before the Germans could freeze her to death. I think now I want to die because to live with this would be far worse. The Germans whipped me for this but did not kill me.

Four women were frozen to death that day along with the woman I killed. Four of the men were Sergeant Muller, Corporal Lam, Private Ritter and Private Hoffman. I do not know the names of the other two but they were private soldiers."

Dan stopped reading. He looked away and then back at the sheet of paper; his mind reeling with the horror of what was written on it. He stood up and walked to the edge of the patio. He knew about the Holocaust, he had studied it. But nothing had prepared him for this.

"It makes grim reading doesn't it?"

He turned to see Colonel Radcliffe placing a tray, with tea and biscuits, on the table.

"It's...Its horrific. I have only read one. Is all this verified?"

Radcliffe picked up the testimony and read through it.

"Yes. There are at least two other accounts of this incident if my memory serves me right. But there are several more just like it. Sometimes they made old women race with boulders on their backs. The losers always died. I seem to remember an incident where two twelve-year-old boys, who were best friends, were made to fight to the death with shovels."

Dan stared at him. He gestured at the boxes.

"Is it all like this?"

"Yes it is. I am tempted to say a lot of it is worse but I think you come to the point where there is no such thing as worse."

Dan looked at him in despair. Radcliffe sat down.

"Why did you come here Sergeant? What are you looking for?"

"I want to find a connection between Bauman and Hoffman."

"Yes but you wanted something more didn't you? You thought you would find the assassin here didn't you? You thought you would find some young girl who had been horrifically treated and who would be motivated to kill. But you won't find one girl with this motivation. You will find several hundred. Everyone who survived Belsen would want to shoot these evil bastards."

Dan sat down.

"I guess you are right. But I think now I have to focus on Hoffman and his associates. Did the SS guards work in set teams?"

"Yes, they were military units. They would be on duty with, broadly speaking, the same group of people every day. The chain of command is similar to ours. At the ground level there would be a Captain, Lieutenant, Sergeant, a Corporal and a troop of men. In the camps the officers would likely to be in charge of more than one troop."

"So how many would be in the troop?"

"There would possibly be only ten or twelve men working in several shifts."

"So this group of soldiers would only have been half a troop."

"Yes but they were off-duty and this was unofficial. When I started interviewing I was hopeful of getting prosecutions in incidents such as this. There was not an officer present so in theory they couldn't use the "I was only following orders" plea. It is hard to believe but technically such individual murders were outlawed by the Reich not that many were ever reprimanded for it."

"So were these men ever brought to justice?"

"No. There were more than 480 members of the SS employed at Belsen. 11, mainly commandants and the highest ranking officers, were hung. 18 were sentenced to prison for periods between 1 and 15 years but all had been released by 1949. More than 200 SS members never even faced a trial."

Dan stared at him.

"That's...That's disgusting."

"It is reality I am afraid. At the end of the war the allies promised they would bring every Nazi guilty of war crimes to justice. And then we had the show-piece Nuremberg trials where 24 men were found guilty of the worst crime in World history. 11 of them were executed. In 1946 the United Nations war crimes committee said that 13 million former members of the Nazi party, including thousands of SS members, were liable to arrest."

Dan could see anger in the man's eyes but he spoke calmly.

"But very few were ever arrested and those that were served very little time. Do you know how many were in prison in 1949, just 4 years after the war?"

"I have no idea,"

"Less than 300. Despite the allies promise to bring everyone to justice, the sum total for a World War that left over 70 million dead were 11 executions at Nuremberg and 300 in jail."

Dan was truly shocked and even unbelieving.

"Surely that is not correct. It is obscene if it is."

"It is true Sergeant. I will tell you a story. When the West Germans took over the prosecutions from the allies they convicted a man of involvement in the murder of eight thousand one hundred people. Do you know what his sentence was?"

"Please tell me he got life-imprisonment."

"No Sergeant. For aiding and abetting in the murders of eight thousand one hundred people he got sentenced to three years in prison. There are hundreds of stories like that. Thousands of men like those in this testimony just drifted back into society. Men who made old women fight and then froze to death the loser, just married, had children, made money and generally lived happily ever after."

Chapter Ten

"But you said you were hopeful of getting prosecutions in this case so why didn't you?"

"Well first of all it wasn't up to me. My job was to record the individual stories and pass them up the line. But it was because of the low ranks of the accused. Even at that early stage it was realized that it would be impossible to bring everyone to justice. If 500 men were responsible for the Holocaust you could jail the lot of them, maybe even a thousand. But there were hundreds of thousands of men guilty of involvement. I recorded all the testimonies I could but I was told that it would only be those accusing officers that would be followed up."

Dan picked up the testimony again and looked at the second page. This had individual identifying marks of the named soldiers. They were very impressive.

"These are really very good. She has the estimated height of the soldiers, their hair color, all facial hair and physical scars. She has even spotted some dental fillings. To note all this when under the pressure she was under at the time is remarkable."

"This was because of a Dutch woman named Gertrud Rep. She was a Jewish lawyer who came to Belsen in 1943. She told inmates to remember all identifying marks on the guards. Very brave Jewish girls who worked as maids in the guard's quarters stole pencils and paper. Gertrud recorded the crimes and the identifying marks. She hid the papers in the stitching of her prison uniform."

"Do you have a copy of those papers?"

"Yes and she also made a diary which I have a copy of. The wording in the original is incredibly small and very brief as she never knew when she would get more paper. She was an incredible woman."

"So she is dead?"

"Just before Belsen was liberated it was massively overcrowded and there was an outbreak of typhoid which killed thousands. She was barely alive. I was told about her and went to see her in the field hospital. I managed just a few words with her but she was in no state to be interviewed. The Doctors told me she would be dead by the end of the day."

"How did you learn about the papers and diary?"

"She got ill a few days before the liberation. She passed them onto the lady you first read about, Klara Schippers, and she gave them to me."

Dan picked up a second testimony, this time by a young Russian girl who had seen her twin sister whipped to death. This time the descriptions of the indentifying marks were not as good.

"It was because inmates from the east were kept in a different part of the camp and never met Gertrud Rep," said Radcliffe.

Dan thought about that.

"If that is the case maybe I can narrow the search down. We know Hoffman was in Gertrud's part of the camp so it follows that Bauman, and possibly Ingrid, were also there."

"That would make sense,"

"But the boxes are in dated order. How do I know which ones contain the right camp notes."

Radcliffe paused before replying.

"The Western Europeans such as the Dutch are in the files marked with a red tab. The Eastern Europeans have a yellow tab."

Dan could sense his annoyance.

"I am sorry. I know how maddening it is when someone destroys your filing system."

"Its fine Sergeant, do as you must. I will retrieve the red tab files. They will probably no longer be in strictly chronological order though."

Dan read through four more files each one as horrific as the last. He took out a note-book and wrote down the names of the soldiers that featured most. After about ten more he had over forty names but a pattern was emerging. A hard-core of six or seven names was appearing more than the others. And one of them was Kurt Hoffman.

"Was this Sergeant Muller ever convicted? He seems the leader of Hoffman's unit. Even by the standards of the SS he seems extreme in his brutality. In fact he appears to be the most evil man I have ever read about."

"He appears more than any other. But no Sergeant Muller was ever recorded as having served at Belsen."

"But how can that be?"

"I don't know,"

Dan stared at him.

"I do. Give me that identifying paper from the first testimony."

Radcliffe did so and then Dan took the Bauman autopsy report out of his brief-case. He stared at both for several minutes.

"It is not conclusive but the size, hair and eye color is the same. Both have a burn scar on the same finger and both identify a silver filling on his upper teeth. The Bauman autopsy has three fillings but he would have aged twenty-seven years by then. Given what you said earlier about it being unusual that Bauman's name did not appear on the testimonies I think it is a safe bet that Muller and Bauman are the same man."

Radcliffe studied both and then laid them on the table.

"I concur,"

Dan looked at him.

"Sir, with all due respect I find it hard to believe that you hadn't considered that."

Radcliffe looked back at him with a blank face.

"When your DCI told me Bauman's name I did consider it."

"If you had mentioned that possibility it might have saved a lot of time."

"Sergeant Coates. Let us get one thing straight. Your DCI asked me to answer your questions and, as a retired army officer, I am duty bound to do just that. But I am not here to investigate these killings. That is your job."

"So you will answer all my questions but if I was to miss something that might lead to the killer would you tell me of it?"

"No Sergeant. I would not."

Dan considered this.

"Can I ask you three more question Sir?"

"Please do,"

"Do you know who the killer is?"

"No I don't,"

"Would you tell me if you did?"

Radcliffe considered this. Dan realized that this man would never directly lie to him at least.

"Yes I would,"

"Would you tell me if you only had a suspicion of who it might be?"

"Sergeant I have a suspicion it could be anyone of about 500 people. All would have a very good motive. I don't think I would waste your time with all those suspicions."

"I will take that as a no then. I have total sympathy for your position Sir. If I had interviewed all these victims I would feel the same way. But I have my job to do."

"So let us get on with it. You will read all the files and I will answer all your questions."

Chapter Eleven

Over the next two hours Dan read over 60 testimonies before he came to one mentioned by Radcliffe earlier.

28th of April 1945
Testimony of Johannes Janssen aged 12
Interviewer Captain Jeffrey Radcliffe
Translator
Paul Van Rooyen
Also present CENSORED
Interviewer's notes

The witness is heavily traumatized and fearful. He is likely to need psychiatric help to get over his ordeal. He would only do the interview if accompanied by CENSORED

"On the 25th of February I and my best friend Ruud De Vries had just finished working in the shoe factory. We were very scared because Captain Hoeness had shouted at Sergeant Muller for bringing him sub-standard workers. Sergeant Muller was very angry and marched all ten of us to an area behind our barracks.
There were four men with him. They were Private Hoffman, Private Ritter, Private Konieg and Private Hadyn. Under Sergeant Muller's orders the private soldiers pulled two boys out of the line and beat them until they were unconscious. Both later died. I do not know their names but I think they were from Belgium.

Then Sergeant Muller ordered me and Ruud to fight with shovels. He pulled his pistol out and said he would shoot us if we did not fight. We fought and when Ruud was lying on the floor and unable to rise I wanted to stop. But Sergeant Muller said he would kill all of my sisters if I did not smash him in the head with my shovel. Sergeant Muller made me do this several times until Ruud was dead.

I am unsure of the date but it was about a week later that Sergeant Muller, Corporal Lam, Private Hoffman, Private Ritter, Private Konieg and Private Hadyn took my sisters Magda, Eva, Karolina, Anna, Ruth and Sarah to a storeroom. There they raped them and then shot them in the head.

Interviewers note.

I have no doubt about the veracity of this last accusation but I have been advised that, because the subject did not witness the event at first hand, it will not be used in evidence.

Dan put down the account and stood up. He felt sick; even dirty.

"Jesus Christ Colonel. How the hell could this have been allowed to happen? I have met Germans. I have played sport with them. They are decent people. But thousands of them were committing atrocities like these less than thirty years ago. And they are still out there somewhere."

"You are going through what we all went through when we discovered Belsen. We have to face the fact that humanity, wrongly directed, is capable of great evil."

Dan sat down and picked up the testimony again.

"Do you know what happened to this boy?"

"I don't know what happened to any of them. I had to develop a level of detachment to be able to do my job. I remember him though. He was practically a mindless zombie. He related the facts with no emotion. It was far from unusual."

"Why was the name of his supporter censored?"

"It was not uncommon. Many refused to do the interviews if they were named and of course, to have legality, they had to be. But there was no requirement for supporters to be named if they didn't want to be. You have to understand that these people, especially the children, were still terrified of the guards, many of whom had fled and were still free. Thousands were dying of disease at that point and a lot of the inmates would like the guards to believe they were dead."

"But that was an irrational fear, surely,"

"It probably was but it would be hard for a child to put their name to a paper accusing a guard, who still terrified them, of rape and murder. And it wasn't totally irrational as the guards at that point would have liked to kill all witnesses. And in the days before liberation they did kill hundreds."

"You said you believed the accusation about the rape and murders. But I thought that sexual relationships between guards and Jewish inmates were strictly banned."

"They were but they almost certainly went on. No one knows to what extent because there are almost no live witnesses. The guards could get heavily punished for it so they almost always killed the victims straight afterwards."

"How would the boy know his sisters had been raped?"

"In Gertud Rep's diary there is a piece about it. That will explain it. A lot of the inmates knew what had happened."

Dan looked down at the stack of unread testimonies and suddenly could not face reading anymore.

"I think I will call it a day Colonel. With your permission I will take these files and the diary with me. I will return them after the investigation finishes."

"That is fine. I will box them up for you. Would you like a glass of brandy before you go? I always think it helps after reading them."

Dan had to drive back to London and he never drunk while on duty.

"How old were the sisters Colonel?"

"I read through Rep's diary last night. The oldest was sixteen, the youngest seven."

Dan looked into the distance feeling bile in his stomach.

"Yes Colonel. I would love that brandy."

Chapter Twelve
Hanover

Sophie leaned back against the side of the swimming pool and watched Klaus Konieg walk out of the changing room. He paused at the edge of the main pool, just a couple of feet from Sophie, and glanced across at the kids in the learner pool.

His gaze lingered for more than was decent but Sophie was not surprised. Before he climbed down the steps he gave an ingratiating smile to a young woman to Sophie's right. The girl stared back at him with a blank face. Sophie glanced away before he looked at her but she felt his eyes on her. It made her flesh crawl.

After getting in he stood by the side of the pool at a right-angle to Sophie. The water was just up to his waist and she saw the shrapnel scar that he had received in Russia across his chest. It was much less vivid now, and his body was fat, but it was clearly there.

She remembered the British officer telling her how brave and clever she had been to remember it. He had told her they would catch him and her evidence would put him in prison or even lead to his execution. Well he was right on one count at least.

She watched him swim away. She knew he would return quickly because this was the end of the pool where he could watch the children.

She waded over to the other side of the pool and swam a few lengths, enjoying the water and the exercise. She couldn't relax but she knew his routine. He would swim, ogle the kiddies, swim again and then more perving. He would leave the pool in 30 minutes. She would leave 5 minutes before that.

Afterwards she could fully relax, for three weeks at least. She had originally planned to take them all down as quickly as possible before they, and the police, knew what was happening. But Sol had advised her to take a break.

And Sol, as usual, had been right. She had been tight as a coiled spring ever since Bauman. If she didn't have a rest she would make a mistake.

Both killings in London had made the newspapers in Germany and it had been suggested that they might be connected. But then the story had been much less prominent. Sophie knew it was because of the discovery of their SS past. The German newspapers knew that their readers didn't want to be reminded of their recent history.

Konieg would have recognized the names of course but it had not caused him to up his non-existent security. She was slightly surprised by this but knew it was because of arrogance, stupidity and denial.

He had accepted the media theory. Bauman had been robbed and then killed because he resisted. And Hoffman had been killed in a brothel. It was a coincidence that he had been in the same unit as both but two random killings in London had nothing to do with him in Cologne. He would know about Mossad but they only killed high-ranking officers.

Years ago she had asked Sol about it.

"Don't they know we might come for them? When they know what they did, how many they raped and murdered, do they never consider someone might plan revenge?"

"They are arrogant Sophie. No matter how hard they see us fighting for Israel some of them will always think of us as sheep being led to the slaughter."

And Konieg was one of them. It is why he didn't hire a bodyguard after the London killings. He couldn't conceive how one of those sheep; one of those pathetic lice-riddled skeletons could ever threaten his life.

She did two more lengths of gentle breaststroke as she remembered swimming with her sisters. Ruth and Sarah had been the best because they were the oldest. Karolina had been better than Sophie and she had hated it even though she had loved Karolina the most. She remembered promising her that one day she would beat her. Karolina had laughed and said it would never happen. And it never did.

After twenty minutes she got out. She saw Konieg leering at the young children. She went to the showers and then changed. Ten minutes later she was sitting on a bench in the park watching the pool doors. Konieg came out right on cue five minutes later. When he was 100 yards from her she stood up and began walking.

She had purposely worn a leather jacket and tight jeans. She could almost feel his eyes on her bottom. She walked a quarter of a mile on the park path and then turned off onto a grass track which led through a wooded area onto the main road. It was a route he used every day.

When she saw no one else around she stumbled on a hidden tree root and went down on one knee.

He rushed to help.

"Can I help my Dear?"

He touched her shoulder and she stood up; grimacing slightly as she put weight on her foot.

"No, I think I am ok thank you."

"Are you sure? I do have medical training."

She looked at him.

"Yes. I am sure but thank you."

There was an awkward silence. He looked nervous as she suspected he always was round adult women.

"Oh good, good. It is not nice to see pretty girls like you hurting themselves. I am Klaus by the way, Klaus Konieg."

She smiled.

"I am Sophie,"

The name meant nothing to him.

He smiled and held out his hand.

"It is nice to meet you Sophie. Maybe I can buy you a drink?"

She kept her voice friendly but ignored his hand as she touched the zip of her open jacket.

"We have met before Klaus."

He gave her a sickly smile.

"I don't think so. I am sure I would have remembered meeting a pretty girl like you."

"Well I was younger then"

"I really don't remember. When was it we met?"

She kept her smile sweet.

"It was in 1945. You raped and killed my sisters."

For a moment he stood there stunned and she pulled the pistol from the shoulder holster. He looked at it, and her, in total confusion. She shot him when she saw the fear.

Chapter Thirteen

Dan had a sleepless night and in the morning phoned his boss and filled him in.

"How do you wish to progress," said Ron.

"I intend to read more of the testimonies today as well as this diary. There are literally hundreds of girls who could be Ingrid and that's assuming she was a survivor. She could well be a child of a victim."

"It sounds like a needle in a haystack job,"

"Yes but I have found numerous links between Bauman and Hoffman. And there seems a select group round Bauman who were especially sick bastards. I would think it likely that, if there is another victim, it would be one of them."

"How big is the group?"

"Probably about seven or eight but I am trying to narrow it down."

"So do we warn them?"

Dan paused.

"I think that would be premature. It is just conjecture right now."

Ron's pause was even longer.

"Yes I guess you are right. And if they have read about Bauman and Hoffman they should be pre-warned of a possible danger anyway. But don't forget Dan, we are dealing with foreign nationals and it is a sensitive time politically what with this common market thing. We have to do things by the book."

"There can't be too many SS men living in England. If there are other killings they are likely to be in Europe. Then maybe we can pass it on."

"I hope you are right but at the moment we have two foreigners murdered in England and we are duty bound to investigate."

"I know the score Ron but you should read these testimonies. Well, actually you shouldn't as they will make you sick. But Bauman and Hoffman were the absolute scum of the Earth. They were utterly depraved."

"I have read many like it Dan. I was a lowly private in the Military police during the war and for a short time I helped with the war crimes investigations. That is how I knew of Radcliffe. How helpful was he?"

"Up to a point he was very helpful but he was very careful with his words. He made it pretty clear he didn't want me to find Ingrid but he would never be deliberately obstructive."

"So he was careful with his words but could never be accused of not doing his duty. Maybe you should remember that."

Dan was surprised and slightly relieved.

"Thanks boss. I will remember that."

"Good but make sure you cover your back because I will sure as hell cover mine. The bottom line is still that it is our duty to find and arrest this killer."

"Ok Boss. I will get started on the diary and phone you later."

Dan got a cup of tea and picked up the plain blue book. On it was printed the words

Diary of Gertrud Rep

English translation copy

25th November 1943
Very cold. Worked in the shoe factory all day
26th November. Recording everyday is a stupid waste of paper.
5th December. My 14-year-old daughter, Lisbeth made a mistake that caused a machine breakdown. Captain Hoeness beat her to the ground and began kicking her in the head. I ran to help and Corporal Lam and Private Hadyn were ordered to beat me. I was beaten unconscious.
6th December. Sergeant Muller came into the infirmary and ordered me back to work. I could not walk so he made me crawl to the factory.
7th December. My daughter Lisbeth died.
8th December. I tell inmates in my barracks to remember all indentifying marks on all guards and officers.
26th December. 11 year-old Jannick Robben was beaten to death for laziness on the orders of Captain Hoeness. We were all made to watch.
1st January 1944. Two elderly French women were made to race naked while carrying heavy boulders strapped to their backs. The loser was strung up, soaked with hose pipes and froze to death. The guards who took part were Sergeant Muller, Corporal Lam, Private Hoffman, Private Ritter, Private Hadyn and Private Konieg. Sergeant Muller announced that it would be a New Year tradition from now on.
   One day I will kill Sergeant Fucking Muller.

Dan continued reading for an hour. It was horrific stuff. There seemed to be at least two brutal murders every three days and at the same time inmates were starving to death and dying of disease.

It was an unimaginable hell but remarkably life, hope and dignity somehow survived. And at the centre of that hope seemed to be Gertrud Rep.

The recording of the indentifying marks was a type of resistance. Most of the adults seemed to accept they were likely to die but they hoped against hope that one day their killers would face justice. This simple act of resistance also seemed to have inspired the children to remarkable bravery.

They stole paper and pencils while knowing they would be killed if caught. And Gertrud Rep recorded all their names in her diary.

She also recorded their deaths.

2nd February 1944. 12-year-old Angelique Kupper and 11-year-old Bette Voss were taken to storeroom number Two and were raped and shot dead. The Guards were Sergeant Muller, Corporal Lam and Private Konieg.

The two girls were heroines who risked their lives many times to bring me paper.

14th March.

14-year-old Katharina Bakker was shot by lieutenant Hessler for theft of paper.

This girl's bravery should never be forgotten and my heart bleeds for her.

Dan read on while marveling at the bravery of these girls and of the woman who inspired them. Up to October 1944 four girls had been shot for theft and there were fifteen allegations of rape and murder. And interestingly they all involved Sergeant Muller and up to five others, one of them being Hoffman.

By this time Gertrud Rep was referring to them as the rape gang.

But now they had hope.

10th October. A civilian worker at the factory whispered to me that the British and Americans were advancing and the Germans were retreating in both the west and the east. I have to be careful with such reports but it is the fourth I have heard in two months.

Towards the end of the diary Dan came to the account of the two boys fighting with shovels.

25th February 1945

2 unknown Belgium boys aged about 14 were beaten to death behind the barracks. In the same incident two 12 year-old Dutch boys, Johannes Janssen and Ruud De Vries were made to fight to the death with shovels. Johannes refused to kill his friend until Sergeant Muller promised to kill his sisters unless he did.

I am now very frightened for his sisters as he is likely to kill them anyway. I no longer believe in God but I will pray for them. Karolina and Anna are incredibly brave and have brought me more pencils and paper than anyone. Anna especially is incredibly resourceful.

1st March 1945.

Today Sergeant Muller, Corporal Lam, Private Hoffman, Private Konieg, Private Hadyn and Private Ritter raped the six Janssen sisters. Sergeant Muller put a bullet into the heads of Karolina, Ruth and Sarah. At that point Sergeant Muller told Private Ritter to take Anna into the other room and to shoot her. He said to be quick as Captain Raedar was coming. Magda and Eva were also then shot, presumably by Sergeant Muller.

Private Ritter disobeyed and raped Anna again. When he was finished Anna somehow escaped and hid in a latrine.

We have to keep her alive. Even in the midst of the horror she did what I told her to do. Even as they raped her she took mental notes. She gave me an amazing description of Muller and the rest right down to their cock size. If we can keep her alive we can convict these at least. They were disobeying orders as they are not allowed to rape us.

But Private Ritter knows the danger and is searching for her. The whole barracks is covering for her but she is spending 20 hours a day in the latrine.

25th March

Corporal Ritter came into the barracks today and this time looked into the latrine. He hasn't been looking as hard lately and he thinks Anna must be dead. Luckily there is much confusion here now as the camp is massively overcrowded with prisoners from the east. Hundreds are dying every day from disease. But he is panicking as liberation is near. He looked down into all 10 openings but we had developed a signal when one of us would tap the floor and my brave little Anna would duck her head under and swim to the other end. Ritter should have ordered us all out before he searched. But private Ritter is as thick as the shit Anna is swimming through.

28th of March 1945.
I have typhoid. My friends tell me I haven't but I know the truth. It is rife in the camp. I just want to live long enough to save Anna. That is what we all want. In a way she is partly dead already. When we can we drag her from the latrine and clean her down before feeding her what scraps we have. She thanks us and is polite but she looks coldly at anyone who gives her sympathy.

10th of April.
The Germans are panicking and some have fled. But those that remain are killing hundreds to try to hide their crimes. Sergeant Muller disappeared several days ago but Ritter keeps coming into the barracks. Today he beat several women but they all said the same. No one has seen Anna for over a month. But he searched the latrines again. I am very weak now but we are told liberation is just days away.

11th April.
Anna Janssen is dead. I thought I was numb to the pain of loss. Death is so common-place here we have become desensitized to it. But Anna's death has affected us all and devastated me. For the first time in nearly two years I have seen people cry over a death. We kept her alive for so long. To

us this little girl was a symbol of hope. But she is gone now. Ritter came searching again and this time he stared at the latrines for ages. He never found her but she drowned. When we pulled her out she was dead. I pray her testimony will bring her killers to justice.

I am close to death now but I no longer care. Now I want to die because Anna Janssen is dead.

Dan could not stop the tears coming to his eyes. As he had read the account he had come to dread the outcome. For over a month this little girl, who had been brutally raped and seen her sisters murdered, had hidden in a latrine.

He had tried to keep his eyes diverted from the next passage as he dreaded what he might see. He had read accounts of over a hundred deaths but, like Gertrud Rep and the other inmates, Anna had come to be a source of hope. And then he saw the words he dreaded. Anna was dead.

He stood up and looked out of the window. He had lost a child. His son was born very prematurely and had died after a week. For some reason his wife Hazel had blamed him and they were separated within a year.

He remembered the pain but the ugly death of a child whom he had never met twenty-seven-years ago seemed to affect him just as badly.

And it was his job to find the woman who was killing the bastards who caused it.

A thought crossed his mind. Where was Anna's description of the rapist's indentifying marks? Surely even with Anna dead it would be powerful evidence and Gertrud would have recorded it.

He went to the box of interviews and found it near the back. Unlike the other folders there were six sheets of paper. On them were the names of the men who had raped and murdered the Janssen sisters and below it were their identifying marks.

It was stunning stuff. The detail was incredible. Every scar and birth-mark was recorded as well as nipple and belly-button shape. As Gertrud had said; Anna had even recorded the size of their penises.

Dan leaned back in his chair and began to feel angry. Anna had died but there were numerous murder charges against these men and this list clearly indentified them. In the midst of unimaginable horror this little girl had recorded every detail and provided overwhelming evidence.

And the authorities had done nothing. Not one of these men had faced a court. After Radcliffe had filed the list had anyone else even read it? Hoffman, and presumably the others, had not even felt the need to change their names.

He put the file down. He had to put his emotions aside and concentrate on the job.

The Muller rape gang appeared in many of the Radcliffe interviews but they were most prominent in the Gertrud Rep barracks. So there must be a possibility that the killer had been there.

He looked at the diary. Gertrud Rep had died at the end of the war but she had given the diary to another lady for safe-keeping. He picked up the very first interview and looked at the name. Klara Schippers aged 44.

It would seem a good place to start. But something niggled at the corner of his brain. He picked up the file with Anna's identifying marks again. He then looked at Klara Schipper's description of Sergeant Muller. It was no comparison of course as Anna had seen much more of his body.

So why, when he was trying to prove Muller was Bauman, had Colonel Radcliffe not given him Anna's description?

He knew why, of course, as Radcliffe had made it clear he would only go so far in helping the investigation. He wouldn't lie and he wouldn't mislead Dan but he would be very careful with his words. So what else had he been careful about? One thing sprung to mind.

He had never confirmed that Gertrud Rep was dead.

Chapter Fourteen

Dan was disappointed to see birds flying over where the camp had been as he had read reports from the original liberators that they never did. He didn't doubt they had told the truth but it would have been very different then.

He had seen the famous newsreels of the piles of skeletons being bull-dozed away by the British soldiers. He remembered too the vacant zombie like stares of the survivors who were little more than living skeletons themselves. Surely no bird then would have dared flown over such a place of death.

But it was different now. Unlike Auschwitz the camp had not been preserved. There was a monument at what would have been the gates but the barracks had gone. There was a new building that Dan knew was a document centre but it looked isolated in the barren landscape.

As he walked towards the building he noticed a larger memorial that he knew had been paid for by some survivors. There were also a number of smaller, probably private ones, dotted about.

As he watched he saw an elderly couple kneeling by a small shrine where they had placed some flowers. The woman was clearly crying and the man had his arm round her shoulders. Dan wondered how often they had visited in the last twenty-seven years.

They weren't the only ones. There were about fourteen other people among the headstones all looking somber. Dan caught the mood. It was a sunny day with a clear sky but there was an oppressive atmosphere about the place.

He walked into the document centre. A young woman at the reception desk looked up at him. She nodded her head in greeting but did not smile. Dan wondered if smiling in this place was even possible.

"Excuse me but do you speak English?"

"Yes I do but not perfectly. How can I help you?"

"I think this is a long-shot but do you have a list of all those who were kept here."

"No. I am afraid not, far from it in fact. The Nazi's kept records but they burnt nearly all of them in the days before liberation. We have a good record of the guards who served here though. They burnt them too but duplicate records were kept at army headquarters in Berlin."

"What about inmates who died here?"

"That is far from complete also as again the records were destroyed. We have had to rely on survivor's testimony and some train records. Some Police records also record people being sent here so we can be fairly sure they died here. We know more about the Belgian, Dutch and German inmates but very little about those transported from the east."

"I think it might be the Dutch I am interested in."

"The centre is split into sectors. The Dutch one is on the far right. It is far from complete but it records all those who died here that we know about. But at liberation time there was a lot of confusion. The camp population was larger than it had ever been and thousands were dying of disease. The Nazi's were also killing hundreds. A lot of names got missed off the lists."

"You said you relied on survivor's testimony for the recordings. Do you happen to know anything about a Lady called Gertrud Rep?"

"Yes, I think I know that name."

The girl walked from behind the desk and led Dan to the Dutch sector. On a table at the centre of the display was a large book. On it were printed the words

A record of many Dutch citizens who were murdered at Belsen
There were many more.

The girl opened it to the first page. On it was a list of the survivor's who had contributed. Third on the list was Gertrud Rep.

The Dutch embassy in London had already confirmed that she had survived her illness at the end of the war. She had been a witness at the trial of camp commandant Josef Kramer who had received the death penalty. The records she had secretly kept had also resulted in the prosecutions of at least ten other officers. The electoral roles also confirmed that she had been alive two years ago.

But nothing had been heard of her since 1946. It was far from unusual but many others, who had done far less than her, had been honored by governments and had been the subject of magazine articles and books. But if she had been asked she had refused them all.

Dan thanked the girl who returned to her desk. He flicked through the pages recognizing some of the names of the dead. He didn't really know what he was looking for or why he had come.

He could not expect to learn anything more from these names than he had from Radcliffe and Rep's diary. No names were going to jump out at him. The fact is the killer could be any one of hundreds.

He was on his way back from Hanover where he had seen the dead body of Klaus Konieg. There was just one bullet in the heart this time but he had little doubt the killer was Ingrid. He had found it interesting that there hadn't been a second shot because maybe that meant there was a potential witness close by.

The Hanover police hadn't seemed interested at all, least of all in an English policeman on their patch. They had taken copies of his case notes for the London killings and had allowed him to continue his investigations on German soil. They had even authorized him to carry a gun. But, while they wanted to share information, they did not want to work in tandem with him. The Female liaison officer, Marita Kaufmann, had been apologetic.

"I am sorry about them. They did not mean to be rude but you must understand how sensitive these murders are in Germany."

"But I have two dead bodies in England and I have to investigate them. I got the impression they would rather I go home and leave them to it."

"But I think we can be agreed that, as any other potential targets are likely to be Germans, it is proper that it is handled by the German police."

"Are they going to tell the press about the SS connection? Are they going to connect it to the killings in England?"

"We will release the details and I expect some newspapers will report it. But I have to be honest. I doubt it will be front page news. Editors and the German people have an unspoken agreement. Very little is written about the SS. It opens up too many old wounds."

"But if I am correct there is likely to be at least three more murders."

"And we will investigate those murders."

"Will you warn them?"

"That is not my decision. Would you want them warned?"

"No, but that doesn't mean they shouldn't be. As police officers we can't allow vigilante law. Or we shouldn't anyway."

"We won't Sergeant. We will try to catch this woman but we must do it in a way that doesn't open those old wounds. If this hits the press in a big way negative stories about our recent past will be in the papers across Europe. There will be more calls for trials and retribution. Germany doesn't need that trauma right now."

Now, as Dan looked at the book of death he wondered if this was right. After Radcliffe had told him about how few Nazi's had served even a small term in prison it seemed that Germany as a whole had been forgiven very easily for the war.

But what was the alternative? There were millions of Germans who were probably guilty of war-crimes. The World could demand massive retribution but that had been tried before in 1918. And, without the German anger at the Versailles treaty, Hitler and the Nazi's would never have come to power.

There was a noise behind him and he turned to see two middle-aged men waiting to read the book. He gave a grim smile and moved away. They didn't return the smile; in fact they seemed to look right through him.

He walked over to the far wall where there was a plan of the camp as it had been in 1945. The right quarter of the camp was designated for Dutch, Belgian and French inmates. Although there was a note saying that "Because of space these designations were not always kept to" Dan thought it likely that this was where Gertrud Rep's hut would have been.

He went to the reception desk and thanked the girl for her help. Just before he left he heard raised voices from the two men. They were pointing at the book and arguing. The girl gave them a disapproving look which they were oblivious to.

Dan's first reaction was to be annoyed as they seemed to be acting disrespectfully in such a somber place. They had also appeared unfriendly to him. But then he caught himself. Who was he to complain when these two men might have lost wives and children here?

He went out and walked to the place where he believed Gertrud's hut would have been. There were markers on the ground but now it was just heath-land.

Dan stood there thinking about all the atrocities that had happened in this peaceful place. Here, where now the sun shone and birds sung, old women had been made to race naked carrying boulders with the loser strung up and frozen to death.

Twelve-year-old boys were made to fight to the death with shovels. Girls as young as seven were raped and murdered. And ten-year-old girls spent six weeks hiding in a latrine before drowning in shit and piss.

He walked among the headstones stopping at names that he recognized and saying a prayer in his head although he had stopped believing in God many years ago.

At the rear of where one of the huts would have been he found three very well kept headstones all with fresh flowers on them. He looked at the first one.

> In memory of Lisbeth Rep aged 14
> who died here in 1943
> A loving beautiful daughter

Amid the later horrors he had read about Dan had almost forgotten that Gertrud had lost her own daughter. He had no doubt that Gertrud had, through her determination to collect evidence, kept many others alive. How had she done all this when she must have been devastated with grief for her own daughter?

He also recognized the name on the next headstone.

> In memory of my best friend Ruud De Vries
> who died at this spot in 1945

How long ago had Johannes Janssen stood where Dan was standing? It was possibly just days as the flowers were still fresh. How often did he come here? How had this boy managed to cope with the memory of being made to kill his best friend twenty-seven years ago?

The third headstone was bigger and he knew what he was going to find on it. Johannes didn't just come here to mourn his best friend.

> In memory of the Janssen sisters who were raped and
> murdered here in 1945

Ruth 16
Sarah 14
Karolina 13
Magda 11
Anna 10
Eva 7

And also their parents
Adler 44 and Gerda 43
Who died at Auschwitz concentration camp
Date unknown

Dan thought again of Johannes Janssen. He had been forced to kill his best friend. A few days later five of his sisters had been raped and murdered. And six weeks later his last sister had died in a latrine.

Radcliffe had described him as almost a mindless zombie and said he needed psychiatric help. And this was before he knew his parents were also dead.

He heard voices and turned to see the two men walking between headstones and still arguing. They stopped at where an old couple were kneeling before a memorial and leaned over them to look at the name on the stone before moving on. Dan was shocked at their insensitivity and the old man looked at them angrily.

Dan looked back at the Janssen headstone and knew he should go straight home. He should drive to the ferry-port at the Hook of Holland, hand in his gun at the police station and then just go. Ron wouldn't object. It was in the hands of the German police now.

But even as he thought it he knew he wouldn't.

Chapter Fifteen

"What the hell are we supposed to be looking for Ritter?" said Ralf Lam.

"I am trying to find out who is fucking killing us."

"Well it won't be anyone in this grave-yard will it?"

"It has got to be some daughter or sister of someone who died here."

"Well that narrows it down to about 50 fucking thousand."

"So, what's your suggestion smartarse? Do we just wait until the bitch kills us?"

"We don't know if she is coming after us. Muller, Hoffman and Konieg acted as a trio a lot of times. It might just be a relation of someone they killed. The bitch has to draw the line somewhere. She can't kill the whole platoon."

"I hope you are right but we did a lot as a six especially... well you know what I mean."

"When did you get so squeamish? Yes I know. You mean the little Jewish whores we fucked and shot."

"For Christ's sake Lam, keep your voice down."

Lam laughed.

"You are still a fucking fairy Ritter. Are you scared of a load of old weeping Jews now?"

Felix Ritter did not reply. He was already thinking he had made a mistake in contacting Lam. He hadn't seen him for nearly twenty-seven years but the mockery had started almost immediately.

Back then it had been much worse. Sergeant Muller had said he wasn't tough enough to be in the SS and the others had taken their lead from him as they always did.

It had all stemmed from his first day at the camp when he had hesitated when ordered to kill a Jewish girl who was about eight. He had done so eventually but the damage was done. He was probably more brutal than any of them after that but he was never accepted and was generally held in contempt.

It was why he had never told them about the girl who had escaped from that last rape. How could he tell them she had bit his penis as he ejaculated on her face and had then run out of the room as he writhed in pain?

That had been a dangerous time on two counts. Sergeant Muller knew these cases could not be passed off as "Carrying out orders" and had said all witnesses must die. Ritter was scared of the allied courts but he was even more scared of Muller finding out he had disobeyed his orders.

So he had searched alone and in vain. It was likely she was dead as hundreds were dying at that point but he couldn't be sure. He had escaped the day before liberation but had been arrested a month later.

He had sat in the stockade with thousands of other SS men for three months dreading the moment he would be taken to an office and charged with rape and murder.

But it never happened. He, like thousands of others, was just released. They were warned they might be re-arrested so he was still scared and not just of the girl. He, unlike a lot of his SS colleagues, did not view his actions as acts of War. He knew he had committed mass murder and could hang for it.

But so had thousands more and he, as a private, was way down the pecking order. He knew this when he read a newspaper article; an article that finally eased his nerves a little.

In it two Jews called Gertrud Rep and Klara Schippers had told how they had informed the authorities about the rape and murder of five sisters. They had then described how the sixth sister had drowned in a latrine while hiding from a guard.

He had initially panicked but had then gone on to read that the authorities had decided that " Because of the lack of any live witnesses, the low rank of those accused and the massive back-log of cases the case would go on record but not pursued."

The girl was dead and he was free and not just from that accusation. The authorities at that point were just not that interested in the lower ranks.

But now, twenty-seven years later someone, who wasn't interested in legal niceties, appeared to be targeting people he had close war-time links with.

But who was it?

"You are right Lam. It could be anyone of thousands. It is like looking for a needle in a haystack."

Lam rubbed his chin while thinking about it.

"I think we can at least narrow it down to the hundreds. We served mostly in the Western Jews camp."

Ritter knew then he had made the right decision to contact him. Lam was an arsehole but he was undoubtedly smarter than Ritter.

"That is good thinking. Let's go to their sector."

As they walked over the man they had seen in the document centre walked past them in the opposite direction. Neither of them paid him any attention.

"Any idea how we narrow it down some more?"

Lam looked round him.

"No I don't."

They walked among the headstones.

"Do you remember any of these?" asked Ritter.

Lam shrugged.

"No, not really, it is all a blur to me. We were just doing what we were told at the end of the day. It was just a job."

Ritter had never believed that. If he was honest he had enjoyed it but he had always known it was wrong. And he remembered too much.

"What do you do now Lam?"

"I am a manager at a construction company owned by my Father-in-law. What about you?"

"I am a caretaker at a school."

"Jesus Christ, they let you near kids. They obviously didn't know what you got up to here did they?"

"I am not like that now. Anyway what do we do?"

Lam thought about it then shrugged.

"Nothing is going to jump out at us here. It could be anyone. We have to be cautious of any woman who looks about forty and tries to seduce us though."

"Is that it? Is that your advice?"

"How many forty-year-old women, or any women come to that, ever approach you Ritter. If one comes up to you and says she finds you irresistible you can be pretty sure she means to kill you."

"You joke, and that is similar to what happened to Muller, but it wasn't like that for Konieg. Aren't you worried Lam? It is probably Mossad."

"I doubt it. Mossad doesn't waste time and resources on the likes of us."

"So it must be someone working alone; someone who was here."

"I agree but who is it?"

"I don't know. If I did I wouldn't have contacted you."

They come to the Ruud De Vries memorial.

"Do you remember this Lam?"

"Not specifically but I remember this though. Six little Jew sisters, isn't this where you lost your virginity Ritter?"

"Fuck off Lam,"

Lam laughed.

"For fucks sake Ritter you must be fifty and you still blush when I call you a virgin. I remember that you were wild for those tight pussies."

"Do you think this is anything to do with what is going on now?"

"How can it be? They are all fucking dead."

"They had a brother called Johannes. I saw it in the documents room. Muller made him kill his best friend."

"Muller and the others were killed by a woman or had that fact escaped you. I can't believe you. There are hundreds of people who it could be and you focus on someone it can't be."

Ritter stared at the headstone. He knew Lam was right but this incident more than any other haunted his dreams; or rather the girl who had escaped had.

He remembered her screaming as her sisters were shot but afterwards, as he raped her a second time just minutes later, she had been unnaturally calm. She had stared at him with hate filled eyes before biting his cock and fleeing. He knew she was long dead but that look still gave him nightmares.

"So your advice is to just lie low and to be careful. Thanks a fucking lot."

Lam considered it for a minute.

"Look you must have contact with some old colleagues. Tell them to keep an ear to the ground and I will do the same. I know we have a contact in the Hanover police who should be able to keep me informed about anything they uncover. That's all we can do but, if we are careful for long enough, she will either be caught or give up. And, as I said, she might not even be targeting us."

"Well yes, that's at least something. Will you call me if you discover anything?"

"Yes, of course,"

They walked back to their cars. Ritter was relieved to be out of the camp grounds but Lam seemed untroubled by bad memories. They shook hands and he drove away.

Lam watched him go and then drove to a nearby rest-centre on the autobahn. He parked by a red BMW. The man in it looked across at him then got out of his own car and joined Lam in his.

"Hello Corporal."

"Hello Hadyn."

"So how was our friend Ritter?"

"He is as big a fairy as he ever was and he is shitting himself right now."

"Did he ask about me?"

"Yes, I told him I hadn't seen you for years."

"Is he right to be scared?"

"No, a member of the SS should not be scared of some Jew bitch. But he is right in that there does appear to be a danger."

"But as you said before it could be anyone of hundreds."

"I think I have narrowed it down and, with your help I might be able to narrow it down a little more."

"What do you want me to do?"

"I want you to find and, if she is still alive, locate a woman called Gertrud Rep. She provided a lot of evidence at the trials and appears to have been a dominant figure in the camp."

"Well I guess she would be too old to be the assassin but you think she might know who it is?"

"It is a bit of a stab in the dark but it is as good a place to start as any. Also, stupid as he is, Ritter might have come up with something. There was a kid called Johannes Janssen at the camp. Apparently we made him kill his best friend and then we raped and killed his six sisters. Rep is more important but I think it is possible that if you find one you will find the other."

"Why?"

"Because the memorial to Rep's daughter is next to the one of the kid's sisters and the one to his friend. They also had the same fresh flowers on all of them. The headstones are all made of the same stone too."

"What do you want me to do if I find Rep?"

"Phone my house and my wife will give you my contact number. But I just want you to observe for the time being. Try to find out if this Johannes is about. I will also give you some witness descriptions of the killer in London. They won't be much good but if you see a woman of the same height and build let me know."

"And if we don't?

"And if we don't then maybe we will have to have a gentle chat with Mrs. Rep."

Hadyn smiled.

"It could be like old times. Did you tell Ritter all this?"

"No, I told Ritter to go home and be careful."

"I am not sure that was the best advice."

"It is shit advice but Ritter is too thick to realize that. The safest thing now is to keep on the move and not to stick to routine."

"You are a ruthless bastard Corporal, you always were. If we three are all on the killers list she is likely to go for Ritter next as she knows where he is."

"Exactly and when she finds him I will find her."

"Do you think that at our age we can handle this Ralf? Maybe we should get some of the young guys to do the dirty work."

"No we can't. Most of them are just stupid skinhead zealots. They quote Hitler's words like a mantra. I don't want them to find out we had sex with Jew bitches as they will report us to the old zealots. During the war we would have got us a severe reprimand but now some of those crazy fuckers might kill us."

"That's a good point. But it has been a long time since I saw action Corporal."

"You are not scared of some Jew bitch are you Hadyn?"

Hadyn was to a certain extent but he was more scared of Lam who he also considered a zealot.

"Of course not,"

Lam smiled.

"Good because I promise you when I find that bitch she will wish she had died at Belsen."

Chapter Sixteen

Dan found Gertrud Rep living less than fifty miles from Belsen just outside the Dutch town of Assen. She lived in a gated community of just three buildings and the telephone beside the locked gate presented him with a problem.

Policemen as a rule liked to turn up unannounced at doors. You could tell a lot from first reactions and the interviewee doesn't have a chance to prepare for what they may be asked. It was the mistake they had made with Colonel Radcliffe. He had known Dan was coming and had worked out what he could reveal and what he rather wouldn't.

And Gertrud Rep was likely to be even less helpful. But, short of lying, he had no choice and phoned the number. A male voice answered and spoke in Dutch.

"I am sorry but I am English,"

"How can I help you?" said the voice after a short hesitation.

"I was hoping to talk to Mrs. Gertrud Rep. I believe she lives at number three."

"Could you state your name and business please?"

"My name is Dan Coates. I am a British Police Officer and would like to talk to her about an investigation."

"Can you hold up your identification to the camera on the wall please?"

Dan did so.

"Can you hold the line please?"

Dan waited two minutes before the voice came back.

"The gate will open now Mr. Coates. You can park opposite number three."

Dan drove up, parked his car and got out. Number three was the smallest of the buildings but, like the security, all were impressive and spoke of reasonable wealth.

There was an intercom beside the door. He pressed the button and a female voice answered at once.

"Please come in Mr. Coates. I live on the second floor or the first as you English confusingly refer to it. There is a lift if you are lazy."

Dan took the stairs and wondered about the lift as it was only a few steps. He got his explanation when he saw the small ramp outside the open door. He knocked.

"Come in Mr. Coates,"

Dan walked in to find Gertrud Rep in a wheelchair. With a blanket on her lap and grey hair she looked all of her sixty-nine years. But there was a vibrancy about her and she had a certain glint in her eye.

She smiled at him.

"Please sit down and I will get us some coffee or would you prefer tea?"

"Either would be fine but please don't go to any trouble."

"It is very little trouble I assure you."

She wheeled herself into the kitchen and he looked round the room. With its photographs of several generations of people it looked like the room you would expect to find in the house of any old woman. Except that Dan knew Gertrud's only child had died at Belsen.

"It is a very beautiful house you have here Mrs. Rep especially the grounds."

"Thank you Inspector but it is not actually mine. It belongs to my neighbor who lets me live here rent free."

"Well it is very lovely anyway. It is not Inspector Mrs. Rep. I am afraid I am a lowly Sergeant."

She laughed.

"I am sorry I prematurely promoted you."

He walked over to the book cabinet but they were all novels and none were about the war or the Holocaust. Dan knew she had been awarded medals by the German, Dutch and Israeli governments but none were on show.

He heard a car drive up and he walked to the window to see a white Mercedes park in the space opposite number two. A dark-haired woman turned off the ignition but then just stared into space for several seconds before resting her head on the steering wheel.

Two young children, a boy and a girl, ran out of number one; their faces full of excitement. The woman got out of the car, smiled and then swooped the young girl up with one arm while embracing the little boy.

A woman in her mid-twenties followed the children out and, when the newcomer put the children down, she embraced her. They spoke for a few seconds and then the young woman beckoned the children inside. The girl obeyed but the young boy, who looked about four, clung onto the newcomers arm.

She turned back towards the car but, as she was about to open the rear door, Dan saw her body stiffen as she saw him in the reflection.

Her head whipped round as she pulled the boy behind her then she stared at Dan with an intensity that shook him. It was like the response of a wild animal protecting her cub. She stood there, her eyes boring into his, poised and ready to strike.

The younger woman said something to her and she glanced at her and obviously asked a question. She then turned her eyes back to him before pushing the boy to the other woman. Then she walked towards the door of number three.

At that moment Gertrud Rep called him.

"Sergeant could you bring the tray through please? It is a bit difficult in my chair."

Dan went to the kitchen and picked up the tray which contained two cups of tea and a selection of biscuits.

"I think I have just startled your neighbor."

"Which one?"

"I think I surprised them both but it is the dark-haired lady who is on the way up."

"That's Sophie. I am afraid you are in for an interrogation. She is very protective of me."

Seconds later there was a rap on the door.

"Come in Sophie,"

Sophie came in. She spoke rapidly in Dutch but kept her eyes fixed on Dan.

"It is alright Sophie. This is a British police officer called Mr. Dan Coates. I think it would be polite to speak English."

Sophia kept looking at him; her body tense and aggressive.

"I am sorry for startling you Miss… Sorry I didn't catch your surname."

She held out her hand.

"I didn't throw it. Can I see your I.D please?"

"He has already shown it to Ronald Sophia."

The hand stayed outstretched. Dan gave her his warrant card. While she looked at it Dan studied her.

She looked tired and wore little make-up but she had attractive features. He would guess she was in her late-thirties or early forties. She looked fit in close-fitting jeans and pullover but there was an animalistic intensity about her that was startling.

But after viewing his I.D she seemed to relax a little. She turned and half-smiled at her neighbor as she returned it.

"I told you not to steal those towels from the Dorchester hotel Gertrud."

"Yes you did. I will be glad to return them to you Sergeant if you will drop the charges."

The woman had lost some aggressiveness but her smile was for Gertrud alone. She looked at him with a blank face and then sat down. Dan turned to Gertrud.

"I am afraid I am here on a much more serious business Mrs. Rep."

"I can guess why you are here Sergeant and please call me Gertrud."

"Oh I see... Well I know how awkward this must be and how uncomfortable this might make you feel. I really do not want to upset you."

"Do you want to arrest the woman who killed two of the SS men who murdered her daughter?" said Sophie.

"Well it is my job to investigate the killings, yes. And there have now been three killings."

Sophie looked at Gertrud.

"Klaus Konieg was killed in Cologne three days ago."

He saw she was surprised at the news.

"Ok, so there are now three dead SS scum. So if you find out who did it you will just congratulate yourself and move on? Is that what you are telling us?"

Her tone was mocking.

"No, of course not. It is my duty to try to arrest her or at least have the German or Dutch police do so."

"So if that is the case how are you not going to upset Gertrud?"

He looked at her and she looked right back.

"You are right of course. But I still have to ask my questions."

"Of course you do. After all you are only following orders."

Dan felt the sting of the words but they also made him angry.

"I appreciate your anger Miss but I have to say that is grossly unfair. The British police are not the SS."

"He is right Sophie. The comparison is obscene and you will apologize. I understand your concern for me but the Sergeant is a guest in my house and you will be polite."

Sophie looked at her then back at him. Their eyes locked for several seconds.

"I am sorry Sergeant. You are both right. I am not going to lie. I do not want you here upsetting Gertrud but it was a disgusting remark."

Dan was surprised to see that she appeared to genuinely regret her words.

"Apology accepted and I will be as sensitive and as quick as possible."

"Right, so if you two have declared a truce maybe we can get on. There is no need for you to stay Sophie."

"I am staying Gertrud. I will sit quietly and say nothing unless I see you upset. But I am staying and that is non-negotiable."

"Ok. The kettle has just boiled if you want a cup of tea. Now Sergeant, ask away."

Sophie went into the kitchen and Dan sat down.

"First of all Gertrud I have to say that it is an absolute honor to meet you. I have read your diary and Colonel Radcliffe spoke very highly of you. Do you remember him?"

"Yes of course. Thank you for your kind words but believe me I have been honored enough."

"Colonel Radcliffe appeared to believe that you had died just after you were liberated."

"I was very close to death. The doctor's called it a miracle."

Sophie came back into the room with a cup of tea and sat down on the settee. She picked up a magazine from the table and started flicking through the pages.

"Gertrud I am going to ask you the same questions I asked Colonel Radcliffe. It would be easier for me if you were completely honest."

"Go ahead Sergeant."

"Do you know who is killing these men?"

"No,"

"Would you tell me if you did?"

"No,"

"Would you tell me if you suspected who was doing it?"

"No,"

"Would you deliberately mislead me if you thought I was on the right trail?"

"Absolutely,"

He glanced at Sophie. She was still reading but she had a half-smile on her face. After her earlier aggressiveness it was a not unattractive look. Gertrud had an amused look on her face.

"Gertrud this is a murder investigation. At the moment just three very bad people have been killed but Konieg was killed in a public place. His body was found by a woman with two young children."

"Sergeant, do you believe I know who is doing this?"

"I believe you will have your suspicions. I think at the very least you might be the one most likely to know."

"Why do you say that?"

"You were the leader in that camp. Your recording of the I.D's and testimonies was a type of resistance."

"I will tell you something Sergeant. If the killer was at Belsen she would have witnessed these men committing acts that you could scarcely imagine. This woman could possibly have seen her Mother frozen to death on a hook after being made to race naked with heavy boulders on her shoulders. She might have seen her brother whipped to death by these men. Her sisters and Mother may have been raped and shot by them. Why would you possibly think I would give her up?"

She kept her voice quiet and her eyes on his but he sensed the anger. Sophie glanced at them both. She was no longer smiling.

"I am sorry Gertrud. I didn't mean to upset you."

"Believe me Sergeant the survivors of Belsen are not easily upset. I am not angry with you but I don't think I can help you."

"Gertrud, I do not want to see this woman jailed. It would be an obscenity. I don't even want to know who she is if I am honest. But if you do know or suspect who it is, tell them to stop. If she stops now the investigation will also stop very soon. We want the case to go away and so do the Germans. But if she carries on we have to carry on as well."

She looked at him levelly.

"You speak wise words Sergeant and, if I knew who it was, I would tell them the same. Sergeant Muller is dead and he was by far the worst, at the time anyway, and so are Hoffman and Konieg. I do not agree with these killings Sergeant. I hated these men more than you would think possible. They have lived thirty-years too long and I am glad they are dead. But I wish this lady had not been so obsessed with revenge that she couldn't enjoy the gift of life that was denied to so many. I wish her hatred had not turned her into a killer."

"Do you think if you did tell her she would stop?"

"I cannot answer that Sergeant as I do not know who it is. I suspect not as she has probably already been told this. Would it make a difference to you Sergeant? What would you have done if for example you had seen, as a child, your Mother gang-raped and then murdered?"

"I would have hunted them down but then I hope I would have given the evidence to police and left them to the justice system."

"The justice system has all the evidence; it has had it since 1945. They have evidence from nearly a thousand people. Only Muller changed his name and there was no need for him to do that. If they wished the police could get their addresses tomorrow. But the justice system is not interested; not at the moment anyway. So when you realize this what would you do?"

Dan looked at Sophie who was looking at him. Gertrud just waited; her face blank.

"I would do the same as she is doing but that does not make it the right thing."

Gertrud smiled sadly.

"You are right Sergeant, it doesn't and I doubt that even if she kills all those she wants to kill it will bring her peace. But sometimes it is not about that. Maybe it is purely about revenge. Maybe this woman made a promise to the loved ones these men killed."

"Do you think that is what this is about?"

She smiled.

"I don't know Sergeant. As I keep telling you, I don't know who it is."

He looked at Sophie who had turned away and was once again flicking through the pages of her magazine. He turned back to Gertrud.

"I don't think I am going to learn anything more here. But I do hope someone can influence her Gertrud. If she keeps getting away with it she will keep doing it until she is caught or killed. I think it is possible she is also putting you in danger."

"I am aware of that. If you thought I could lead you to her it is possible others might as well."

"Doesn't that worry you?"

"Would worrying change it? I also have a level of security here."

"Ok but please take care. I very much admire your conduct in the camp. I was especially moved by the way you tried to save the girl called Anna."

Dan was immediately aware of a new tension in the room. Gertrud's expression froze and the flicking of the magazine pages ceased. Then Gertrud smiled sadly.

"That was a great tragedy. For six weeks the whole hut fought to keep her alive. It was all we cared about."

"When I was reading your diary I was praying she would live. Are you still in contact with her brother?"

"What do you want with her brother?"

It was Sophie who spoke and now her voice was one again aggressive. Gertrud fixed her with a look.

"Calm down Sophie. The answer is yes Sergeant but he is of no interest to you and I would prefer that you took my word for that. Johannes was very damaged by the camp. I hate to call it mentally disturbed but that is probably accurate. We are very protective of him. We couldn't save his sisters or parents but we will do our best to protect him."

"I understand that but when you say "We" what do you mean? Are you still in contact with a lot of survivors?"

"Yes, I am in contact with quite a lot. Some I see quite regularly but some I only write to as they live quite far away."

"Would that be in Israel?"

"A number do live in Israel."

"Please do not be upset by my next question but I have to ask it."

"Go on,"

"Is Johannes Janssen especially close to any female survivor aged between thirty-four and forty-two?"

Gertrud was silent and just looked at him. The whole interview she had been relaxed and in control but he could see signs of tension now.

It was Sophie who finally spoke.

"I would fit that description. Johannes is a friend of mine."

He looked at her. The hostility was still there but it was under control. She looked at him directly with almost a challenge in her eyes.

"When you say friend what do you mean?"

"It means we are not lovers."

"And you are a survivor of Belsen?"

"Yes,"

"Can I ask your surname?"

"You can but I don't see why I should tell you."

"Stop being so ratty Sophie," said Gertrud. "Her name is Sophie Visser. Her Parents died at Auschwitz."

"I am very sorry to hear that."

"Just ask your questions Sergeant and spare me your sympathy," said Sophie. "Or actually I will save you time and just answer the one you really want answered. When Muller and Hoffman were killed in London I was in Benidorm in Spain. I stayed at the Silver Sands Hotel. When Konieg was murdered I was in Majorca staying at the Medusa hotel. Johannes was with me both times. Does that make any other questions redundant?"

"What were you doing there?"

"Buying hotels or shares in them at least."

"I never actually said you were a suspect."

"But you have been thinking I might be ever since I walked through the door. Is that not true?"

"No, the thought actually crossed my mind when you saw me in the reflection."

"You seem very ready to jump to conclusions."

"You are right but the conclusion I jumped to was that you reacted like a well-trained soldier. Have you spent time in Israel Miss Visser?"

"Yes. I was educated in Israel and attended the University of Tel Aviv. And yes Sergeant, I spent time in the Israeli army. It is a legal requirement."

"Is Israel now your home?"

"No Holland is. May I ask why you are still asking me questions when you know I am not the woman you are chasing?"

"I won't know that until I have checked your alibi."

"That is a fair point."

"I am intrigued by your friendship with Johannes. I find it surprising he travels to business meetings with you. Is he an employee of yours as well as a friend?"

"That is really none of your business but Johannes enjoyed it as a holiday. He and I were children together living in hell. Both our families are dead. Why is it such a surprise that a friendship built in such circumstances should remain strong?"

"You are right. I am sorry. It was an insensitive question."

"That is alright Sergeant. Were there any other questions?"

She looked completely calm now. All aggressiveness was gone but Dan was aware it could resurface in an instant. He gave a rueful smile.

"Well there was one but I would fear for my life if I asked it."

He stood up.

"I thank you both for your time. There is one other thing I would like to mention. It is probably nothing but I don't think it would do any harm to tell you."

"What is it?" said Gertrud.

"On the way here from Hanover I stopped at Belsen. While I was there I saw two middle-aged men. Their behavior was strange to say the least. They seemed rude and disrespectful. I wouldn't have expected survivors, or family of survivors, to act like that there."

"It is not all that unusual. Most tourists who visit are respectful but not all. Anti-Semitism did not die in Germany with Hitler Sergeant. But I take your point. It could have been SS men trying to get a lead like you were. Thank you for telling us."

"Well good-bye and thank you for your time."

"What were you going to ask me Sergeant?" said Sophie.

He smiled while inwardly cursing himself.

"It is not important and I don't think you would like it."

He opened the door.

"Sergeant ask me the question,"

She stood in the middle of the room; her face stern and her hostility returning.

He forced a smile but felt his face redden

"I was going to ask if you were free for dinner,"

The fact that Gertrud Rep burst out laughing probably saved him.

Sophie looked completely shocked but then anger and outrage quickly followed. She opened her mouth but Gertrud's laughter stilled her. She looked at her and at Dan and, for the first time since she walked into the room, looked unsure of herself.

Then to Dan's great relief he saw she was trying not to smile and, try as she might, she couldn't quite manage it. In the end, although there was still some anger, she accepted defeat. It was a rueful smile at best but it was a smile.

"No Sergeant. I am not."

Chapter Seventeen

Dan phoned his boss from his hotel and filled him in. He also asked him to get all he could on Sophie Visser.

"Do you expect the alibi to stand up?"

"I am pretty sure you will find her name on the register of both hotels. She seemed very confident and she also appeared surprised to hear of Konieg's death."

Ron gave a little laugh.

"I see you are following Colonel Radcliffe's advice and choosing your words carefully."

Dan felt a bit embarrassed.

"I am just trying not to head up a blind alley. I have no evidence against her beyond the fact she appears to be the right height and roughly the same age."

"Did you get anything from Rep?"

"No. I suspect she has an idea who is doing this and she will try to stop them. But there is not a chance in hell she would give her up to us."

"Do you think Radcliffe knows?"

"I doubt he knows but I think he could probably narrow the search down considerably if he wanted to. I am going to phone him later as I have a few questions for him. How long before we leave this to the Germans?"

"We can't for the moment I am afraid. We are getting political pressure. It appears some people at the top would like to embarrass the German government by revealing how many Nazi war criminals are still walking about as free as a bird."

"It is pretty shocking."

"I agree but that is not our problem. I will get the information you want. Call me tomorrow."

Dan ended the call and then rang Radcliffe.

"Hello Colonel. Does the name Sophie Visser mean anything to you?"

There was a pause.

"I do not think I interviewed anyone of that name."

"That wasn't my question Colonel."

"The name does ring a bell yes. I believe she is on the list of survivors."

"Can you tell me if she was the unnamed supporter when Johannes Janssen gave his testimony?"

"No I cannot tell you that Sergeant. A promise was made to that person and I intend to keep it."

"Do you know why Sophie did not give an interview?"

"No but many didn't. As I told you before many were still scared of reprisals from the guards and some were just traumatized."

"But who took the final decision that they wouldn't be interviewed?"

"There were some professional people there but mainly it was some of the older survivors. They were very protective of the children, especially the orphans."

"Why do you keep all the records Colonel?"

"At the moment there is no appetite for charging these men. But at some point in the future that may change. I doubt it to be honest but I feel I owe it to the victims to keep their testimonies. Most of these men have not been officially cleared. They were released but told they could face future arrest."

"But could they still not use the "I was only following orders" plea?"

"At Nuremberg that plea was rejected but I suspect for the lower ranks it would still carry a lot of weight with a jury."

"But in some cases, like rape, they could not use it."

"Yes, but as I said before, rape victims did not live to tell the tale. Where are you going with this Sergeant?"

"I don't know really but I would love the people who raped and murdered the Janssen sisters to face justice."

"Believe me, so would I, but I doubt that will ever happen."

"But Anna survived for some time and the guard called Ritter knew the danger. But he never knew for certain that she had died. He must have been scared after the war."

"He would have been. But I believe a couple of adult survivors told a newspaper about the case. They were disgusted that the authorities weren't going to prosecute because there were no live witnesses."

"Was one of the survivors Gertrud Rep?"

"I think it was yes,"

"The same Gertrud Rep you led me to believe was dead."

"I think I said I was told that she would be dead by the end of the day. The truth is Sergeant I didn't want you bothering her. She is a remarkable woman and has suffered enough. I am also fairly sure she was little help to you."

"No she wasn't and I agree that she is remarkable. Colonel, this is a direct question. What do you know about Sophie Visser?"

"I know she is a very wealthy woman. I also know she has financially supported many of the Dutch survivors of Belsen. Beyond that I know little. I have attended several memorial events and spoken to others about her but she has never attended."

"Do you know she was in the Israeli army?"

"No I didn't but that is not surprising. Millions of Jewish survivors made their home in Israel after the war. If this young lady was educated there she would have had to do several years of National service."

"Do you know how she made her money?"

"I was told she was very successful in investment banking and share dealing. Another survivor said she had made a fortune in property development. She appears to be a very successful and resourceful businesswoman."

"Do you know if she ever married?"

"No, I know nothing of her private life."

"Ok Colonel. Thank you for your time."

The next morning Dan had breakfast on the verandah of the hotel and tried to decide his next move. The night before he had written down all the facts he had. It hadn't taken long. The truth was he had very little.

But, despite this, he felt close to a break-through. He would have missed something. He would have heard or read something that set off an alarm bell in his sub-conscious. It would come to him. The trick was not to try too hard to access that information.

At that moment he saw Sophie Visser in her white Mercedes stopped at a junction just in front of him. She looked at him and when the light turned green she moved off and parked down the street. A man got out the passenger door and she said something to him before walking over to Dan.

"Good Morning Miss Visser. Can I get you a coffee?"

"Thank you Sergeant but I can get my own."

"Please. I insist you put it on my bill."

Before she could refuse Dan waved to a waitress who came over and took the order. Sophie sat down.

"Thank you Sergeant."

"Please call me Dan."

"No, I am comfortable with Sergeant."

"Is that man Johannes Janssen?"

"Yes and no I am not going to allow you to speak to him."

"You seem very confident that you could stop me."

She ignored that.

"Why are you still here Sergeant?"

"I am considering the best form of action. One choice is to remain here."

"Do you think one of those men you saw will turn up and threaten Gertrud?"

"They might be completely innocent but I think it is a possibility someone may turn up."

"And then when they do you think it entirely possible your killer will turn up as well."

"She may already be here. It would be the logical step."

She smiled.

"I am leaving today Sergeant."

He smiled back.

"But you have an alibi. I am surprised you are going though. I really think it possible Gertrud may be in danger."

"I think you over-estimate that danger. The time when SS men could come into a foreign country and murder old women is gone. I am relieved you no longer think I am a suspect."

"I didn't actually say that. I said you had an alibi. Just because someone booked into those hotels using your name doesn't mean it was you."

"That sounds a bit far-fetched."

"Not for a rich woman or a Mossad agent."

"You are correct on the former and way out on the latter. I see you have been checking up on me."

"Yes. After the most horrific childhood imaginable you have done very well for yourself. I understand you have also helped other survivors who have not done quite so well."

She looked at him for several seconds.

"I know you mean well Sergeant but I am not comfortable with either sympathy or praise. I have just played the hand that fate dealt me."

"Who were those children I saw you with?"

"They are the grand-children of a friend of Gertrud's. She survived Belsen but died ten years later. The woman you saw was her daughter."

"Did you never have children yourself?"

"You are being very nosy Sergeant. No, I have never had children and I have never married. I really do advise you not to ask why."

Dan cursed himself as just days before he had read that many women from the concentration camps, because of malnourishment and disease, had never been able to conceive.

"I am sorry Sophie. I can be an insensitive idiot sometimes."

Just for a second her mask dropped and he sensed deep sadness. She gave a half-smile.

"I forgive you as you are just a man. And when did I allow you to call me Sophie?"

He smiled.

"I got fed up with you setting all the rules."

Her smile was a bit fuller this time.

"Do you have children Sergeant?"

"I had a son but he died within days. He was very premature. I was divorced soon after."

"I am very sorry. It appears I can be insensitive too."

"It was a long time ago."

She smiled sadly as she stood up.

"I have to go. Good luck Sergeant."

"May I ask where you are going?"

She smiled.

"It is just a business trip."

He stood and shook her hand.

"Could I ask you to think about what Gertrud said Sophie? I mean about the killer not finding peace even if she achieved all her aims."

She looked into his eyes.

"I am aware of Gertrud's thoughts on the subject. Can I also give you some advice?"

"Yes, of course."

"Go home Sergeant. Go home and forget you ever met me."

Chapter Eighteen

Ex-Corporal Lam kept the binoculars trained on Ritter as he left his work shed at the school. Then he scanned the surrounding area to see if anyone else was spying on the caretaker. It was his second week of watching and so far he had seen no one.

He fought against the feeling that he was wasting his time. Both he and Hadyn were on the move and hadn't been at home for three weeks now. The killer could not know where they were. If all three of them were on her list she had to go for Ritter first.

But they may not be on the list. There had been numerous times when Muller, Hoffman and Konieg had acted alone. Maybe the killers grudge was just against these three.

He again wondered who it could be while knowing it was useless. He had probably killed about fifty people while at Belsen. The first few had shaken him but, by the end, he was hardly giving it a second thought.

He had tortured, raped and shot children. It had become a game for the guards; a contest to see who could come up with the most humiliating ordeal and then death. He didn't remember a single face or name.

He hadn't seen them as people; they were just vermin.

After the war he saw it was wrong and he often wondered how he could have acted that way. But he couldn't honestly say he regretted it. It was the best time of his life and he still hated Jews.

The fact that Israel had been allowed to come into existence had proven Hitler right when he said there was a World-wide Jewish conspiracy. The fact that no American president could get elected without the Jewish vote backed that up.

Himmler was right when he said that only the SS had the stomach to do what the white Christian World knew had to be done. And even though that World condemned them the fact that they never pursued the vast majority of the SS after the war proved they knew it was right.

But it was not politically correct to say as much. This was why there had been little in the press about what, essentially were, serial killings. It was also why he knew the police would be dragging their heels and hoping the case would go away.

If the killer was after him he would have to stop her himself.

He turned the glasses back on Ritter. Lam was on a hill about a mile from the school that was in the base of a valley near the medieval town of Bamberg. The school was surrounded by trees but Ritter appeared to be avoiding the thicker wooded areas. If maintenance was needed in these areas he did it in school time when there were children around.

Ritter was obviously on high-alert. In the two weeks Lam had watched he had hardly been seen alone. He would be vulnerable doing his job in the early morning or late afternoon but, even during these times, there were teachers and pupils getting in early or staying late.

At night he stayed in his house which was on the school property. Lam had never seen a visitor and he presumably kept it locked and secure.

His only trips in his car were to the local supermarket in town on a Saturday. And each time he had gone at 12 noon when the place was packed.

Lam was trying to put himself into the mind of the killer and he couldn't see how she could kill Ritter without massive risk. The killer would also be aware that a murder at school would lose them sympathy and could result in a media frenzy.

He scanned the perimeter again. It was mid-afternoon now. He had decided that this would be the last day he would search during the 9 until 4 school day. He would come in the morning and the late afternoon.

Then he would give it another week before suspending his vigil. Maybe that was what the killer had already done. Maybe she had seen it was impossible at this stage with Ritter on high-alert. She would wait for him to relax and to think the danger had passed.

He focused his glasses on the three spots he thought it most likely the killer would be hiding. These were the spots where the woods were closest to the perimeter fence. Two were only 300 meters from Ritter's house. The third was further away but across the playing fields and away from the main school buildings.

He studied all three for a good five minutes but saw nothing. All three had possibilities but there would be huge dangers for a killer. She would have to get to the house unseen, somehow force entrance and then escape.

This was why he had discounted a fourth point. This had trees as close as ten meters to the fence and the wood was at its widest point from the road. But it was on the other side of the school from Ritter's house; possibly a half mile away.

He turned the binoculars on it meaning to give it a brief scan but then, as he was about to look away, a movement caught his eye. He looked for it again. There was nothing but, no, there it was. There was a movement a few yards into the woods. There was a figure behind a tree.

It was probably just a dog-walker but he kept his eyes focused on the spot and he saw no dog. The figure moved out slightly and his heart-rate rose as he saw it was a woman. She had a black cap on but he could see shoulder length blonde hair.

She glanced up and he could see more of her face. He was too far away to be certain of her age but she was clearly female and the right height if the London witness statements were to be believed. And she was undoubtedly acting suspiciously.

She came to the edge of the woods and he saw that she had something in her right hand. She was at the bottom of the school playground where there was some five-a-side football pitches. At this point the pitches were empty but Lam knew there would be children playing football in the last hour of school which was only fifteen minutes away.

The woman glanced up at the school and then stepped out into the open. She walked quickly to the gate in the fence which was about twenty meters away. He didn't understand what she was doing. The school was packed with kids. She had no chance of reaching Ritter's house unseen and he wasn't there anyway.

She reached the gate which was locked but then he realized she had a jemmy in her hand. She forced it into the side of the lock and, with her feet tight against the fence, broke it. The gate swung open but she pulled it closed and put some kind of padding in the side to give the impression it was still locked. Then she casually walked back into the woods.

Lam was mystified. It was clear she intended to enter here when the school closed but there were at least three other points of entry that were much easier and safer. And she had also miscalculated as there was to be another lesson on the pitch and someone was bound to notice the damaged lock.

But then it hit him. That was what she wanted. The teacher would see the broken lock and would inform the caretaker about it. And Ritter would be expected to fix it by the next day. After the kids had gone home Ritter would be forced to come to this vulnerable spot alone.

Lam stared into the binoculars but the woman was gone. His heart was beating fast now and the time was near. When visualizing this moment he had thought he would have time to plan; to prepare. But it was now. The woman intended to kill Ritter probably within two hours.

And by then he had to be in a position to kill her.

He wondered if he could do it. It had been twenty-seven years since he had killed someone and they had been defenseless. It had been thirty years since he had fought and killed in Russia. And in Russia he had been young.

This woman was far from defenseless. She had already killed three times and her plan for Ritter showed how clever and resourceful she was.

Or maybe not; maybe she had under-estimated how scared Ritter was. Maybe he would find an excuse not to do the job until tomorrow when there were people around. But then Lam realized he was making excuses himself. He was trying to find a reason to avoid putting his life at risk.

Of course it didn't matter if Ritter came. He wasn't here to kill Ritter. But the woman was and she would be there whether he came or didn't. And so Lam had to be there too.

He had to go through with it. The fact she had come for Ritter probably ensured he was on her list as well. He would never have a better chance of ending this.

And he had got the drop on her. His plan had worked. He was smarter than the Jewish bitch. All he had to do was go into the woods and creep up on her as she waited for Ritter to appear. She would be caught totally unawares. He would walk up behind her and blow her brains out.

He watched as the kids came out to the pitch. He searched for the woman in the woods but she was nowhere to be seen. It was about twenty minutes before he saw a young boy beckon his teacher and point out the broken lock. The teacher looked at it and told the boys to play on.

Lam moved now. He calculated it would be at least forty-five minutes before Ritter was informed of the broken lock and it would be another twenty minutes before he could get to the scene.

He guessed that the woman would like to be in position in about fifty-five minutes. He needed to be at the road side of the woods by then.

He rushed to his car and took the gun out of the glove compartment. He had had it for years but had only acquired the silencer a month ago. He started the car immediately; trying not to think about what was to come.

Chapter Nineteen

It took him about thirty minutes to find the road. He was tempted to park up and wait but the woman would be looking for potential witnesses and a man sitting in a car alone would scare her off. He drove towards the end of the road and saw a telephone kiosk. He turned at the T junction and parked in the next street.

He waited twenty minutes. It was the longest twenty minutes of his life but in the end the time was going too fast. He was trying to control his nerves and looking for an excuse not to act. The temptation to start his car and leave Ritter to his fate was almost overwhelming. But if he did this it could mean his own death in the near future.

When the twenty minutes was up he looked in the rear-view mirror and reminded himself that he was an SS soldier. He was the best of the best and more than a match for a fucking Jew bitch.

He got out of the car and walked round the corner to the phone kiosk. There was a man in it but that wasn't a problem. All he needed was a reason to be standing on the road. After five minutes the man left and Lam went in and picked up the phone.

Two cars came down the road in the next five minutes but none stopped. He looked at his watch. Surely the woman should be getting into position now.

Then he saw a small green Volkswagen turn into the road. It slowed and parked about two hundred meters away. At the same moment he became aware of a woman waiting to use the kiosk.

He turned his back to her and whispered some gibberish into the phone as he watched the car. No one got out for a minute. The woman outside tapped the glass. He looked at her and she pointed to her wrist-watch impatiently. He turned back to see the woman with the blonde hair going quickly into the woods.

He ended the call and brushed past the impatient woman outside while trying to keep his face hidden. She made a derisive noise and stepped into the kiosk.

He walked slowly towards the Volkswagen and glanced inside to check it was empty. He looked back at the phone kiosk but the woman was looking the other way. After one more glance in both directions he stepped into the woods.

There was a sort of path but he could see the outline of the school buildings anyway. He walked slowly and tried to avoid walking on branches. He took out his pistol and held it under his jacket. As the trees thinned out he went even slower looking both left and right.

He knew he was very vulnerable now but even if the woman saw him first he didn't think she would shoot straight away. She probably had a photo of him but there was no way in this semi-light, and at a distance, that she could be sure it was him.

And she wasn't hunting him. It was Ritter she was focused on. She had no idea that Lam was within a 100 miles of this place. If she saw him she would think he was a passer-by for a time at least.

He was sweating now and his heart was beating wildly but then he saw her. He stopped and gripped the gun harder. She was thirty meters away kneeling by a tree and partly concealed by a bush.

She was about ten meters from the perimeter fence and over her head Lam could see the gate. He looked at the path in front of him trying to see thin branches or twigs. Then taking a deep breath he advanced another ten meters.

How close did he have to get? In the distant past he had gone to a firing range but not for years now. And this was a live target. He knew he had to kill her with one shot or at least put her down. He couldn't allow her to scream. He decided he had to be as close as five meters at least.

He took three more careful steps. The desire to rush was overwhelming but he knew he had to resist it. This woman had already shot three SS men. If she heard him and turned at this distance she would win in a shooting contest.

But she showed no sign of turning. All she was focused on was looking for Ritter. Lam hoped he would come. If he appeared she wouldn't take her eyes off him.

He took seven more steps that seemed to take five minutes. He took the gun out and pointed it at the woman's back. But he was still 10 meters from her. He took one more step then froze as he saw the blonde hair twist slightly to the left. But she was only moving her position to get a better view of the playground.

He waited until she settled and then took two more slow steps. He paused; his mouth dry and took one more. He stopped and tried to breathe evenly. His hand was shaking slightly as he sighted on her back. He took one more step. He swallowed and the noise seemed loud in his ears but the woman didn't turn.

He was now close enough to see the tiny movements of her shoulders. He would take two more steps and then he would fire.

He took the next step then stopped. His heart missed a beat as he heard something behind him. It was something almost intangible; like a breath.

He turned his head slowly; keeping his gun pointing at the woman.

Behind him, barely a meter away, with a gun in her hand, was the woman from the phone kiosk. She looked at him with a blank expression on her face. He stared at her; frozen in place. They looked at each other for three seconds at least. The expression on her face did not change.

Then the silencer on the gun moved a millimeter and for the merest fraction of a second Lam felt a blinding pain in his head.

And then he knew no more.

Chapter Twenty

Sophie stepped over the body and whispered loudly at Joe.
"Come now, quickly,"
He looked at her
"He's coming, he's coming. We can take him now."
Now she hissed at him.
"Get here now, that's an order."
He turned and run to her.
"But he's right there we…"
"Shut up. Pick him up; just a little."
He did so and she kicked his gun underneath the dead body.
"Now come with me and take the wig and cap off. Put your arm in mine and walk slowly."
They walked slowly back through the woods.
"Look happy. We are meant to be lovers,"
They stepped out onto the street. Sophie saw a man walking his dog about a half-mile down the road but he was too far away to get a good look at them.
They got in the car. Sophie would rather have driven as Joe was agitated. But it wasn't usual for a woman to drive a man and people noticed the unusual.
"Pull away quickly Joe as I don't want that guy to get our registration number. But then drive steadily."
They drove to the T-junction and turned right.
"Carry on as we planned Joe but keep it steady."
He ignored her and she knew he was sulking. They drove without speaking until they came to the track that led into the

thick forest. They drove up it until they came to a clearing where there was a barn which they drove into.

They parked and got out. Sophie changed the number plates while Joe prepared the Jet-washer. Ten minutes later the green Volkswagen was white and they drove back to the autobahn.

It was another ten minutes before Joe broke the silence.

"We could have done it. He was right there. He was coming. I saw him."

"Joe where was he exactly?"

"He was on the play-ground?"

"Was it the upper or lower level?"

"It was the upper but he would have been there in a minute, two at the most."

"No he wouldn't Joe. He would be cautious. He would know how vulnerable he was and he might even expect it to be a trap. He would have been at least five minutes and as soon as he saw me he would have ran. We didn't have time Joe. There was a dead body behind us. It was never a feasible plan. Lam should have realized that."

Joe stayed silent. Sophie braced herself.

"We have to face something else Joe"

"I am sorry."

"That's not good enough. You disobeyed an order Joe. You promised me that you would do exactly as I said without hesitation."

"I am sorry...but he was right there. I won't do it again."

"You put us both at risk Joe."

He was silent for over a minute.

"I am really sorry. You know I would never want to put you in danger."

She put an arm on his shoulder as she knew he was upset.

"I know you wouldn't Joe but you did put us both in danger."

"Please let me stay with you. I helped you. I mean I did well didn't I?"

He was right.

When Lam and Hadyn could not be found at their homes she had decided to check out Ritter. It was when she saw the position of the school in the valley that she wondered if the others were using him as bait.

It was entirely possible as he was always the outsider of the group. She remembered the others laughing at him and calling him a virgin.

She had looked at the countryside and decided on the best spots to spy on the school. There were several but out of laziness, arrogance or sheer stupidity Lam had just chosen the most obvious; a local beauty spot with a café and benches.

And then she had just sent Joe to the cafe to make sure Lam had observed her breaking the school lock.

"Yes Joe, you did amazingly well and you held your position bravely in the woods. Lam could have risked a shot at anytime. I am proud of you but we can't ignore what happened afterwards. I might leave you to guard Gertrud next time."

"Please. I need to be with you. I promise it won't happen again."

He was frantic now and on the verge of tears. She stroked his hair.

"Ok Joe. Calm down. I will think about it. You know I would want you more than anyone else if it was possible."

She sat back in the seat. In truth she had no intention of dropping Joe. She should of course, and she knew Mossad could provide her with a more reliable partner. But Joe would see it as a betrayal and he was one of only two people in the World she would never betray.

She knew how to handle him; she always had. He would be better next time because she had made him aware she was disappointed in him. And he deserved to be there as these men had destroyed her beloved older brother.

After the war people had told her that she was lucky that at least one sibling had survived. But the Johannes she had loved before the war had not survived. The Johannes that her and her sisters had all teased had not survived.

The Johannes who would punch her and make her cry, but who would beat up any other boy who did so, had not survived. He was a shadow of that Johannes; a husk. Right from the day Belsen was liberated he had been totally dependent on her.

But she loved him because he was the only member of her family she had left.

"I wish he had suffered more. It was too quick. He should have known who you were. He should have known why he was to die."

"There was no time Joe. It was too close to the road. I would have preferred it that way but it doesn't matter that much. They just have to die. That is the important thing."

"What about Ritter?"

"We might have to put him on hold for the time being. He will be very hard to get to at the moment."

"So do we go after Hadyn now?"

"We have to find him first. The man Sol has watching his house says he hasn't been seen for weeks."

"So do you have no idea?"

Sophie thought of Dan Coates and his concerns about the men at Belsen.

"I have a few possibilities."

"Well you guessed right about Lam."

"That was a bit lucky. He just did what I would have done."

"So what would you do if you were Hadyn?"

Sophie thought about it and then lied.

"I don't know,"

"So where are we heading?"

"We will head for Assen but my plans may change."

He smiled at her

"I think you want to see that English policeman again."

She smiled at his expression as it stirred a memory of the old Johannes teasing her as a child.

"I am not going to have a romance with the man who wants to put me in prison Joe."

"I think you liked him."

"I like a lot of men."

He laughed.

"No you don't. You once said all men apart from me are complete bastards."

She smiled.

"I was exaggerating just a little. You take me too literally at times Joe."

But he wasn't too far out. She had grown up to be deeply distrustful of men. In her mind men used women so she in turn had used them.

It was Ritter who had taught her that men could risk all for sex. Ritter had disobeyed a man he was terrified of because of an overwhelming sexual desire. She had learnt the lesson well.

She knew she was damaged of course. Normal women didn't sleep with men purely to learn about corporate takeovers and the granting of building contracts. Most women weren't so obsessed with making money that they shied away from normal human relationships.

But then most women hadn't seen their sisters raped and murdered and were bound by a promise to avenge them whatever the cost.

She thought about the Englishman. She had to admit he had got under her skin somehow. She liked the way he had been gentle with his questioning of Gertrud although she was being as unhelpful as she could be.

Sophie had been hostile and rude but she had admired how he had stood up to her. And that strange quip about a dinner date. It had completely blind-sided her which rarely ever happened. She had been amused by it and by his clear embarrassment at having said it.

It had been stupid and dangerous to speak to him the next morning. Even now she couldn't believe she had been so irresponsible. It was clear he still suspected her and she had gone on to confirm she was leaving. Now, when he learnt of Lam's death she would go right back to the top of his list of suspects.

What was even more worrying is that she had no clue why she had risked it.

"Pull over at that phone kiosk Joe,"

He did so and she phoned a number.

"Bamberg Police. How may I help," said a man's voice.

"There is a dead SS man in the woods behind the rear fence at the Franz-Ludwig school,"

She ended the call and got back in the car.

"Why did you do that? It will mean they will be on our tail sooner."

"We are far enough away now and they can't do much until the morning. I didn't want a child to find the body."

They drove a bit further and then Joe again broke the silence.

"When I said "What about Ritter" I meant will you make him understand who you are and what he is about to die for?"

Sophie remembered, as she often did, the nativity play her, Johannes and her sisters had put on for her parents every Christmas morning.

"Yes Joe. I will make sure he understands."

Chapter Twenty-One

"This Sophie Visser is quite a character," said Ron after Dan had phoned with an update.

"Is that good or bad?"

"That would depend on your perspective. She is very well known in the business sector. She has been head-hunted by a number of investment banks and she is considered quite brilliant and incredibly resourceful. But other less complimentary words were also used to describe her."

"What words?"

"Well bitch came up a lot. Unscrupulous bitch, cold bitch, disloyal bitch and manipulative bitch were just a few. She has cut quite a swathe through the city of London. She has also been investigated for insider share dealing although nothing has ever been proven. She seems to have a knack of investing heavily in stocks that shortly after go through the roof. Some think that she gets this information by sleeping with the right people."

"But she has never been charged."

"I have a friend in the City of London police who interviewed her under caution. He said she was quite a looker, very intelligent, fearless and the hardest woman he had ever met. Then he phoned me later and said he was wrong. She was the hardest person he had ever met; period."

"I suppose when you have been imprisoned by the SS a British bobby is not going to intimidate you too much."

"I suppose so. He actually quite admired her although he suspected she was guilty. There were a few positive comments from some women who have worked under her. She never socialized but she tended to treat the girls from the typing pool better than most. But the general view is that she is a stop-at-nothing ruthless bitch with no morals."

Dan had ended the call and thought about the description of her. She had been called, ruthless, fearless and as hard as could be.

And this was the woman who had once been too scared to give an interview to Colonel Radcliffe.

But was Radcliffe telling the whole truth? It still bothered Dan that he hadn't shown him the extensive indentifying marks supplied by Anna Janssen before her death. And he had also done something out of character when Dan decided to only look at the files from the Western Jews.

He had said they would no longer be in strict chronological order. But there was no reason why they wouldn't be. Why did this meticulous man not take them out in order? Was it because he didn't want him to find Anna's descriptions of these men?

And what about Gertrud Rep? Although she had admitted she would cheerfully mislead him he couldn't say for certain if she had done so. He picked up Gertrud's war-time diary again.

He read through it and found nothing and then read through it again. On the third time he saw an inconsistency. It was very tenuous but it was there. The last few entries were too long.

For two years her entries were short and concise; they had to be as she never knew when she would get more paper. Even the death of her daughter had received only a few words.

In those last few entries she also writes that she is on the verge of death. But at that point the Germans were still in control. She would have been worried about the diary falling into their hands. It would have been destroyed which would have been a disaster as it contained proof of multiple war crimes.

So why, when she was so desperately ill, had she written in such detail rather than quickly pass the diary on to Klara Schippers to ensure its safe-keeping after her death?

Chapter Twenty-Two

Franz Hadyn was nervous as he dialed the number. He had called Lam's hotel twice before and both times he had been told he was out. It wasn't like Lam to deviate from plans. The agreement was that Hadyn would phone at seven in the evening for an update and orders. But Lam had been out two days on the trot.

The receptionist answered on the second ring
"Hello Castle Hotel, how may I help?"
"Could you put me through to Mr. Ralf Lam's room please?"
There was a short hesitation before she answered.
"Just one moment sir,"
There was another pause before a man's voice came on the line.
"How may I help you sir?"
Something was very wrong.
"I am trying to reach a Mr. Ralf Lam."
"Could I have your name please sir?"
Hadyn instinctively knew he was talking to a policeman.
"Why do you need my name? Where is Mr. Lam?"
"Could I ask how you know Mr. Lam?"
Hadyn put the phone down and tried to keep a lid on his panic. There were two choices. Lam was either under arrest or dead.

If the police were involved there might be something in the German newspapers. But he was stuck in Holland. Who was he to phone?

He thought of Lam's contact in the Hanover police. He had met him a week ago as, on Lam's instruction, they had met up and the policeman had supplied Hadyn with a police ID card. But he didn't know his name or how to contact him.

He decided on an old SS colleague from Hamburg who knew Lam and might also know the police contact.

"Hello Helmut. I am in Holland at the moment. None of the boys have appeared in the press in the last few days have they?"

"Did you know a guy called Felix Ritter?"

Hadyn's heart missed a beat.

"Yes... Yes I did. What about him?"

"Well a dead body of a fifty-five year-old-ex-soldier was found in the woods behind a school in Bamberg three days ago. I made some enquiries at the local branch and Ritter works at the school as a caretaker."

"But the police haven't confirmed it was him yet?"

"No which leads me to believe it is. They would have gone public earlier if there hadn't been an SS connection. Was Ritter fifty-five?"

"I think he was younger than that. I think it might be Ralf Lam."

"Why would you think that?"

Hadyn remembered Lam's warning and wondered how much he should tell him.

"Lam told me he was going to see Ritter."

"Do you think Ritter killed him?"

"There would be no reason why he would."

"In that case this has to be linked to those other killings. Were Bauman, Hoffman and Konieg in your unit?"

"Yes they were."

"So you must be shitting yourself right now,"

"It is pretty fucking worrying, yes, I have a family."

"Do you have any idea who is doing it?"

"Lam came up with something which is why I am in Holland. We wiped out a family but a boy survived. But it is a woman doing the killing. Lam thought this old Jew bitch who was a sort of camp leader might know something. But it is a bit of a stab in the dark. The truth is it could be anyone of hundreds."

Helmut laughed.

"You left too many of them alive Hadyn. We had a rule at Treblinka; if we killed one family member we killed them all."

"It was a lot fucking easier in the east and everyone who was sent to Treblinka was scheduled to die. In the camps in the west we had to abide by a few more rules. No one gave a fuck about Slavs but people were more sensitive about the French and Dutch."

"You may be right but I don't see how I can help you. I could get some guys but where would we start looking?"

Hadyn knew he had a point but he also knew he would be reluctant to help in any case. There were a few real SS zealots who still thought the war was going on, but most just paid lip service to their old oaths of loyalty to each other.

They might hide him, get him out of the country and help him with funds. But they wouldn't put themselves or their families in danger.

"I wasn't looking for help. I was just trying to find out about Lam."

"How do you plan to interview this old woman in Holland? It is a bit risky doing it the old-fashioned way."

"I know but it might have to come to that if I think she knows anything. Lam had an idea I am going to try but it is getting to the stage that I have nothing to lose. I need to smoke this bitch out."

There was a pause before Helmut answered.

"Hadyn, did you guys rape anyone?"

Now Hadyn hesitated.

"Of course not, it was prohibited."

"I know but we all know it went on. I will take your word for it but if you raped someone and left them alive I would put them top of the list. Or maybe look for a daughter or sister of a woman you raped and killed. Some women are a bit touchy about rape."

It was a good point but they had killed all the women they had raped; Muller had made sure of that.

"I take your point Helmut but, like I said, I didn't rape anyone."

Helmut laughed.

"Well maybe you should have done. We can probably hide you for a while or get you to South America if you want. It will take some arranging but there are loads of the guys down there."

Hadyn had been thinking about it but it was a horrible prospect. It would mean up-rooting his family and possibly never being able to come home. He also knew the Nazi communities in countries like Chile were run on strict military lines. He was a private and the thought of, at 53, being bawled out by a sergeant did not fill him with glee.

"Thanks Helmut but that is not a road I want to go down if at all possible."

Hadyn ended the call and then walked back to his hotel. He sat on the bed and considered what to do. Strangely he wasn't scared which was a double-edged sword. On the one hand it enabled him to think clearly but it could also mean he was under-estimating both the danger and his enemy.

He had to fight against it. Lam had under-estimated her and it would appear that he was now dead. Lam had used Ritter to smoke her out. He was going to follow Ritter to see who else was following him. It had seemed a good plan. So what had gone wrong?

The answer was obvious. The killer knew what Lam looked like while he knew absolutely nothing about her. So Hadyn's first task was clear: He had to indentify the bitch.

He remembered what Helmut had said about the rape victims. He knew there were no live witnesses but a lot of survivors would know what happened to their relatives. He thought about the rapes.

 He had been involved in about eight if he remembered correctly. But he hadn't killed any of them. Muller allowed Lam and Hoffman to kill some but mostly he did it himself to be sure they were dead. But then a memory came to him.

The six sisters.

He remembered that a few days before they had made two boys fight to the death with shovels. And when one of them refused to kill the other Muller threatened to kill his six sisters. And then afterwards he had thought it would be funny if they raped and killed them anyway.

How sick they had been. But by that time raping and killing children was almost second nature. Now he could see how evil it was but at the time he had not given it a second thought. They were just Jews after all.

That had been the last time. Shortly afterwards Muller had disappeared and the allies had arrived. Hadyn had got away but had been arrested just a week later.

At that time the Allies seemed determined to charge all SS guards with war crimes. He had been told to just keep saying he was only following orders. That was why Muller had insisted on all rape victims being killed as this plea would not cover rape. And Muller had shot all the sisters himself.

All except one.

Hadyn sat back as he remembered. Muller had shot several of them but one of the younger ones was going crazy. The Captain of the watch was about to do his rounds so Muller ordered Ritter to take her into the next room and shoot her.

But Ritter had been beside himself with lust as he had just lost his virginity. He had probably had a second go at the girl before he killed her. There had been a shot. Surely he hadn't let her escape?

No, of course he hadn't. If the girl had lived Hadyn would have been questioned about the deaths in his post-liberation interrogation. And he would possibly have spent a lot of time in prison. He might have even been hung. No, the girl was dead but it was possible a relation of hers was behind the recent killings.

He remembered what Lam had said about the brother, Johannes Janssen. He was the boy they had made fight and would clearly have the motivation. Was it possible he was working with a female assassin; an assassin from Mossad?

It might be nothing to do with the rape of the sisters of course. It probably wasn't but he had to indentify the killer anyway. That was the number one priority and his only hope of doing so was by gaining access to Gertrud Rep's house.

Chapter Twenty-Three

Felix Ritter checked all the doors and windows were locked again. It was the fourth time he had done so in the last hour. He sat down. He felt sick with fear.

He knew a police car was parked just 100 meters away but it did little to calm his nerves. He knew the two officers were not there primarily to protect him. They had made that clear enough. They were there to catch the killer as it seemed clear that Ritter would be a target.

But they had made the point that the assassin was highly unlikely to make it that easy for them. And they wouldn't be there for more than a week. He had begged for more protection but had got little sympathy. The officer who had interviewed him had been brutally honest.

"The public would not like us spending their taxes on protecting an SS camp guard Mr. Ritter. I served in the Afrika Corps under Rommel and I think you and all the SS are a fucking disgrace. You have dragged the honour of the German military through the mud. I will do my duty and try to catch this killer and this may keep you alive. But, if I had my way you would all have been strung up in 1945."

They had asked him about Lam and the others and then they had got onto what he had done at Belsen. He had been tempted to tell them everything, even about the rapes, but he knew he couldn't. He had never been officially cleared of wrong doing and was always liable to arrest. In the end he had just admitted to being a guard. The officer had smiled at him.

"In that case you have nothing to worry about Mr. Ritter. If you have just done your duty and not committed crimes against the inmates no one is likely to have a grudge against you."

Ritter had hated him and he didn't understand. The guards had to be brutal as anything else was seen as weakness. If he was seen as a Jewish sympathizer he would have been severely punished and sent to the Russian front.

Did Lam try to set him up? It was the only thing that made sense. Lam had watched him to see if the killer showed herself. And she had and now Lam was dead.

But if that was true it also meant she had been watching him as well. And she had killed Lam less than half a mile from Ritter's door. And she might still be close. The police had said she was probably miles away but why would she be? No one had a clue who she was or what she looked like.

The sensible thing to do was to leave; to disappear. He even knew how he would do it.

He would go to a Bayern Munich football game. He would enter one turnstile with thousands of others and then leave at another. No one could follow him in a crowd like that. And then he would jump on a train to the other side of Germany.

He could change his name and cut off all contact with his previous life. He could even get the SS veterans to help him as they had done the same for hundreds of others after the war. They also had a fund to help him financially.

But as soon as he thought it he realized that it was a pipe-dream.

The SS would ask why he had never been seen at the commemorations of Hitler's birthday or at the anniversary of the beer-hall putsch. They would ask why they should give him money from a fund that he had never contributed to.

Ritter was a coward. He had known it since he was about 5-years-old and his life had been a constant struggle to hide this weakness.

At school his best friend had been a Jewish boy called Gustav. They did everything together. But when everyone joined the Hitler youth he had joined too. Two weeks after joining he had, along with a baying crowd, thrown bricks through the window of the tailor shop owned by Gustav's father.

He would always remember his friend staring at him, with tears in his eyes, as he did so.

He had felt dirty but after the Hitler Youth he had joined the SA because they were the strongest force in Germany. And when the SS became the dominant force he had joined them.

But he had never felt he belonged and he knew his colleagues suspected he was an outsider. Sergeant Muller had seen it straight away. He remembered that first killing at the camp. The 8-year-old Jewish girl was staring up at him with innocent eyes. He had felt revulsion but with Muller looking for any sign of weakness he had pulled the trigger.

He had killed many more after that but he had never been accepted. And when the war had ended where once being a member of the SS was a point of pride now it carried a sense of shame. Many had stayed loyal. Ritter had dumped them instantly.

But now he could not go to them for help; indeed it would be positively dangerous to do so. So if he was to disappear he had to do it himself.

But that was hard. His mother and sister still lived close. If he run the killer would watch them. He would never be able to contact them again. And he didn't have enough money to start a new life.

And he was scared. He would feel horribly exposed if he left. For the moment there was a degree of safety in staying put. The police believed that the killer would not approach when there were kids at the school. They said he was probably safe anywhere if he wasn't alone.

But, while he could lock himself in the house after school time, that wasn't sustainable in the long-term. In a month's time the kids would be on holiday for 6 weeks and he would be alone at the school.

And how long would the danger last? Surely it would only end when she was caught but the police had no idea where to start looking. He was also well aware that they just wanted the problem to go away.

He felt like crying. He didn't deserve this. He wasn't like Muller, Lam and the rest. He had been forced to do the things he had done. He hadn't enjoyed it; in fact it had sickened him. But he had had no choice.

He took the Luger pistol from underneath the cushion of his chair. It gave him some comfort but he knew it was dangerous to have it. If the police saw it he would be arrested and he would certainly lose his job.

He had had it since the war but it was only a week ago that he had taken it from the attic and cleaned it up. He couldn't carry it during the working day with kids around but he would at all other times.

The phone rang. He picked it up expecting it to be his Mother.

"Hello Ritter,"

He was wrong.

"Hadyn,"

"I take it that the body out there was Lam?"

"Yes, how did you know? Did Lam set me up?"

"He didn't set you up. He just thought that if the bitch went after you he would spot her."

"So you knew about it. Thanks a fucking lot."

"Don't get mad. He didn't intend you to be killed."

"I don't suppose he intended to be killed either but that's what happened."

"Alright, stop shitting yourself. I have a question for you and tell me the fucking truth."

"What question?"

"That last session with those six sisters. Muller told you to take that girl into the other room. Did you follow his orders exactly?"

Ritter hesitated.

"Yes, yes, of course I did."

Hadyn screamed his reply.

"You stupid cunt, you didn't did you?"

"Stop panicking Hadyn. It's not her. She died in the camp."

"How do you know that?"

"I read it in the paper. Two Jews were complaining about six sisters being raped and killed and about the fact the allies weren't going to pursue the case because there were no live witnesses. They said five of the girls had been shot and the sixth had drowned in a latrine while hiding from a guard."

"And you were the guard I suppose."

"Yes I was."

"How the fuck did she get away from you? She was only about 10-years-old. Or were you just too fucking squeamish to kill her?"

"For fucks sake Hadyn this is an open line. Look, she just bit me and run off. And anyway it doesn't matter as she is long dead."

"It might matter. She lived long enough to tell her tale and would have indentified us. Do you remember the name of the Jews who wrote the article?"

"Yes, one of them was that woman who appeared at Nuremberg."

"Gertrud Rep,"

"Yes, that's it."

"I am about a half-mile from her house as we speak."

"Do you think she knows something?"

"I think it's possible. The fact she wrote the article suggests she is very bitter about this case. Lam also thought it was probable she was still in contact with the brother of the six girls."

"She is hardly likely to tell you even if she did know."

"She will fucking tell me. I promise you that."

"Be careful Hadyn. It is not 1943 anymore."

"Ritter don't you understand. If we do nothing we will die. The police don't give a fuck and we have no idea who it is. You might sit in your house waiting to die but I am fucked if I will. You always were a cowardly shit."

Ritter felt the old accusation hit home. He was surprised by how much it still hurt but he reined in his anger. He needed Hadyn to go through with his fool-hardy plan.

"Look, I am just saying be careful. Can you imagine the shit storm if an SS man was discovered torturing a Dutch Jewish woman?"

"Yes, I know what you are saying Ritter. You want me to save your bacon while you cower in your house. And I will because I also want to save mine. Goodbye Ritter."

Hadyn ended the call before he could reply. Ritter put down the phone. Despite the abuse he had been glad of the call. It hadn't really lessened the fear but Hadyn had a plan at least.

He walked to the window. The police car was still there. He sat down and remembered the girl as he often did.

She had stared at him as he raped her. She had been calculating and working on a plan to escape even then. What kind of 10-year-old could be that detached? How could a girl that age outsmart and outfight an SS soldier?

But that girl had died in a latrine. That girl was not the one hunting him. But that fact was of little comfort and he held the gun tight.

Chapter Twenty-Four

"Hello, this is Police Inspector Rainer Strauss of the Hanover police. I would like to speak to Miss Gertrud Rep if that is possible."

"Just one moment Inspector"

Hadyn waited by the phone at the gate. He felt nervous but he was in control. He was more excited than anything. Hadyn missed the war. It was the only time in his life that he had felt truly alive.

In the years since he had done a series of boring jobs. He wasn't particularly intelligent or ambitious and he was constantly overlooked for promotion. He was just a worker; a drone.

But once he had been important; once people had been terrified of him. People got on their knees and begged him to spare their lives. Once he had had the power of life and death over people. It was a heady feeling and he had never found anything that come close to replacing it.

But maybe today he could have it again.

"Could you put your ID card up to the camera please Inspector?" said the guard's voice.

Hadyn showed his fake ID. He was committed now as he knew if he was caught using it he would end up with a prison sentence. The guard studied it for at least 30 seconds.

"Ok Inspector, I will open the gate. Miss Rep is at number 3. She is expecting you."

Hadyn walked up the drive. He was tense now. Would she recognize him? He thought it doubtful. He knew he had not aged well. He was considerably heavier, wore thick glasses and sported a bushy mustache. When he saw old photos even he found it hard to believe this young clean-shaven Adonis was actually him.

And he would not have stood out at Belsen. He had no doubt that modern courts would consider him a brutal criminal but there had been far worse guards than him. Muller and Hoffman would have been hard to forget but Hadyn had just been one of many.

He pressed the buzzer at number three and a woman speaking German answered him.

"Please come in Inspector and go up the stairs. My door will be open."

Hadyn already knew she was disabled as he had been watching the compound for a week. He knew the comings and goings of all which is why he had chosen the late afternoon.

She smiled up at him as he entered. She looked frail and vulnerable in the wheelchair.

"Please come in Inspector. Can I get you a coffee?"

"That would be nice thank-you."

She wheeled herself into the kitchen and he took a look round the room. He saw several pictures of women around the age of the killer but they could have been anyone.

"Can you give me a hand Inspector?"

Hadyn brought the coffee and biscuits in and then sat down.

"I can guess why you are here Inspector. I had an English policeman interview me a few days ago. I am afraid I wasn't much help."

Hadyn had been told this by his police contact. He could guess how friendly and accommodating the Englishman would have been. He would take a different line.

"We are aware of that Miss Rep but we were not satisfied with the answers you gave him. I don't think you realize that we are dealing with a serial killer here."

She looked a little taken aback.

"I am sorry Inspector but I can only tell you the truth. I do not know who is killing these people."

"Are you aware that another man has been killed in Bamberg?"

"Yes, they released the name this morning."

"And did you recognize that name?"

"I knew a Corporal Lam at the camp, yes."

"And I am guessing you hated him. Am I right?"

She looked at him for several seconds. She seemed baffled by his question.

"I was an inmate and he was an SS guard. Of course I hated him."

"Do you hate him enough to protect his killer?"

She looked nervous now but at least she didn't lie.

"Yes Inspector but I do not know who the killer is."

"But that is my point. Why should I believe you?"

"There is no reason why you should but how do you know I am not telling the truth? There are hundreds of people it could be. I did not know everyone at the camp."

"You see I find your answer interesting. You say "People" when it is known the killer is a woman. Why would you do that other than to broaden the list of suspects? And if you are willing to mislead me on that what else will you mislead me on?"

"I find your line of questioning aggressive Inspector."

"And I find your testimony bullshit Miss Rep. You may not know who is doing this but I am willing to bet you have an idea. Please tell me who you suspect?"

She looked scared now. He had deliberately made his interview sound like an interrogation to try to bring back long-forgotten memories.

"I really have no idea. Please believe me."

He slammed the table causing the coffee to spill.

"I DON'T BELIEVE YOU,"

She tried to wheel herself back.

"STOP WHERE YOU ARE"

She stopped. Hadyn could see she was trembling slightly.

"Please, you can't do this. I am a Dutch citizen. I have rights."

"Fuck your rights, this is a murder investigation. I cleared this visit with the Dutch police. And if I tell them to arrest you for shielding a murderer they will do so."

"You are lying, you can't do this."

"And what if I am lying, what the fuck are you going to do about it?"

She looked at the phone by the wall. He sneered.

"Don't even think about it. I would tip you out of that fucking chair before you get anywhere near it. Now tell me the truth."

"I...I don't know anything. You have to believe me."

He looked at her and then slowly brought out a pistol from inside his jacket. Her eyes widened as she watched him put it on the table. Then, keeping his eyes on hers, he stood up and took a hunting knife from his belt. He sat down and looked at her.

"Now tell me the truth. Who is it?"

She looked shocked now as well as scared.

"You are not the police,"

He sneered at her again enjoying her fear.

"Well aren't you the intelligent Jew? No I am not the police. I am your worst fucking nightmare. Now tell me what I want to know or I will start to cut bits off you."

"You... you can't get away with this."

"Well maybe you are right but it won't do you any good will it? Don't you understand bitch. I am a desperate man. If I don't find out who this is I will die. Now tell me."

She looked at him and then at the knife. She was clearly terrified but he saw the trace of stubbornness in her eyes. She would try to hold out and hope for rescue.

"I...I can't tell you what I don't know."

He sighed. He had hoped it would be easier. But he had always expected resistance. He stood and picked up the knife.

Chapter Twenty-Five

The German policeman was at least honest.

"Ritter was no help at all. He is not going to admit to doing anything illegal as he thinks we will arrest him. But that leaves us at square one. Basically every female survivor who was at Belsen is a suspect. How did you get on with the Rep woman?"

"She was no help."

"Do you think she knows anything?"

"Yes, but she is never going to admit that. Are you going to interview her?"

"There doesn't seem much point. We can't make her tell us anything and a German policeman bullying an old lady who survived the Holocaust is not going to go down too well with the public."

"How hard are you trying Inspector?"

"We have had to step it up a bit after Lam. Speaking as a guy who served honorably under Rommel sergeant I hate the SS scum as much as anyone. But the last murder took place near a school and Ritter is a school-caretaker. We can't ignore that."

"I don't think she will hit him at the school."

"It would seem rash and the fact she told us where Lam's body was suggests not. I am not going to ask you any other questions about why you think that. If I did so I might begin to suspect your talk with Miss Rep wasn't as unproductive as you suggest."

"Gertrud Rep told me nothing that was helpful Inspector. What are you doing now?"

"We have a car outside Ritter's house and we are interviewing a few ex-guards and inmates. It is not much good as it is in the interests of both groups to tell us nothing. What are you going to do?"

"Well I have been told to stay on the job for a while. We think that Ritter and Hadyn could be the only other targets and you have got Ritter covered. We don't know Hadyn's location so I might as well stay here."

"He wouldn't be stupid enough to go into Holland and threaten Rep. If I was him I would be on the first plane to South America."

"The killer is also likely to lay low for the time being Inspector. Ritter is protected and Hadyn is hiding. She has no time limit on this. She might wait for a year or two before she comes back for them."

"That is true but that is not how serial killers usually work."

"I don't think we can think of her as a normal serial killer. She has waited 27 years so what would a couple more mean?"

The Inspector laughed.

"You are right sergeant. We might never know who this lady is and, I have to be honest, that would suit me down to the ground."

Dan ended the call and thought about the Inspector's last words. They might be true for him but they weren't for Dan. He already knew who the killer was.

He left the hotel and walked towards Gertrud Rep's house. He knew he was on very dangerous ground. At the moment he could still claim to have no real evidence and he was confident he could survive any professional misconduct charge.

But the fact remained that a woman had murdered 4 men in 2 European countries and he had a pretty good idea who that woman was. The only responsible thing to do was to report his suspicions to the German police.

It was a very uncomfortable position to be in. He remembered his training; No matter your personal feelings the bad guys are always the ones that break the law.

But while that was fine in theory it wasn't so easy in real life. He knew who the good guys were here and it wasn't Hadyn and Ritter.

But there was more to it than that. No one, apart from their families, would lose any sleep over the death of the SS men but what if an innocent witness was killed? What if a policeman was killed?

It was the point he was going to make to Gertrud Rep.

He used the phone on the wall and after a few seconds the security guard answered.

"It is Sergeant Coates to see Gertrud Rep. I was here a few days ago."

"Yes I remember. I think you should co-ordinate with the German police a bit better."

"I am not sure I understand you."

"Well there is a German policeman with her now."

That was weird.

"Are you sure, they told me they weren't sending anyone?"

"Yes, an Inspector Strauss is with her,"

Dan felt a shiver run down his spine.

"Open the gate now,"

"I have to inform…

"Open the gate now. I think Gertrud is in danger. Open it now."

"But..."

"That man was not a cop, open the fucking gate."

"Oh shit," said the man as the gate opened.

Chapter Twenty-Six

Hadyn approached the trembling woman with the knife in his right hand. He held it inches from her face.

"Just tell me and save yourself a lot of pain."

Her voice was little more than a whisper.

"I don't know, truly I don't know."

"Look, maybe you don't know but you must have a suspicion. Just give me a name and I will leave."

He could see she was thinking about it but then she gritted her teeth.

"I don't know, honestly I don't know."

He moved the blade close to her right eye. She watched the tip warily. She looked beside herself with fear.

"Miss Rep. If you don't tell me what I want to know I am going to gouge your right eye out. You have 5 seconds."

She shuddered. Hadyn knew losing sight was a primeval fear. It was a much more effective threat than death. The woman looked like she might faint but again he saw a setting of the jaw.

"I don't know who is doing this."

Her voice was a little stronger at this point and he could detect defiance. The woman had accepted she was going to die. He put the blade at the corner of her eye. She closed both eyes and waited for the pain.

"You see, now I know for certain you are lying. If you weren't you would have made up a name at least."

He stepped back and sat down in his chair. He put the knife down and picked up the gun.

"So it seems we will have to go for the nuclear option. The time is quarter to 6 Miss Rep. And what happens at 6?"

Now he saw real terror in her eyes.

"Please... please don't do this."

He smiled.

"Yes Miss Rep. At 6 every night those sweet little children from next door come calling. They jump out of their car and while their mother goes into her house the 2 little cherubs come to see their Auntie Gertrud."

She looked round in panic but she was helpless.

"Now Miss Rep. You might not be bothered about losing your own sight but what about that little boy's? How old is he, 4 or 5?"

He went silent and let the tension grow. The clocked ticked loudly. The woman looked sick. Then she made a decision.

"Her name is Sophie Visser."

"And where is this Sophie Visser now?"

"I...I don't know."

"You are going to have to do better than that. How do you contact her?"

She hesitated.

"The clock is ticking. You have 10 minutes before I rip out the boy's eye."

"I have a number I can call. I think it is a hotel. Then she calls me back."

"Does she call back in under 10 minutes?"

"Sometimes....but not always. She might be out."

"Well you better hope she does. Phone her now."

She wheeled herself to the phone and dialed a number. He stood by her.

"If you say anything that I think is a warning the kids will pay a heavy price."

The phone was answered. The woman spoke quickly.

"My name is Gertrud Rep. Could you ask Miss Sophie Visser to ring me as soon as possible. Tell her it is very urgent."

She ended the call. Hadyn smiled at her.

"So now we wait,"

He was enjoying himself but he had a major decision to make if the woman didn't call in 10 minutes. It was pointless to harm the children if she didn't ring. The threat had worked and he had a name. If she didn't call he would tell Rep to send the children away. But he had to leave within 15 minutes. The longer he stayed the more danger he was in as the security guard made regular calls.

But it was a different matter if she did ring back.

They waited in silence before the tension got to him.

"So was this Sophie Visser in the camp as well?"

"Yes she was,"

"She should have let bygones be bygones. It was just war. And the men she killed were just privates. We had to do what we were ordered to do."

The woman just looked at him. She was clearly terrified and sick at the thought of her betrayal but he could see a trace of contempt in her eyes. Then the phone rang.

The woman's eyes widened at the sound and he picked up the gun and leaned in close.

"Answer it,"

Rep picked the phone up slowly.

"Hello, Gertrud Rep's residence,"

There was a second's pause before a woman's voice came on the line. It sounded bright and breezy.

"Hi Gertrud, how did your check-up go?"

"The Doctor said they found a tumor on one lung but they had it under control. Sophie.... We..."

Hadyn snatched the phone from her.

"Ahh Miss Visser, I believe you have been looking for me."

There was a short silence. When she spoke he could hear the fear.

"Who is this?"

"Well it is not Felix Ritter so that should narrow it down. Where are you exactly?"

"What have you done to Gertrud?"

"She is fine at the moment. So she has cancer. That would probably explain why she still didn't give you up even when I was about to gouge her eye out."

He looked at the old woman and gestured with his gun.

"Move back,"

The woman wheeled her chair back a little.

"Don't go anywhere near the door. I asked you a question Sophie."

"I... I am in Munich."

"Do you know why she gave me your name Sophie?"

"Please. I am in Munich. Please leave them alone. I can meet you."

"So you do know. How perceptive of you. Now, if you don't tell me the truth I am going to do to those kids what I told Rep I was going to do. Maybe before I take out their eyes I will cut off their genitalia."

"Jesus Christ, no."

He laughed.

"If you remember me from the camp you know I will do it. We have to meet Sophie as the kids will never be safe. It is not as though you can go to the police? You have murdered 4 men. Now where are you?"

"I am in Hanover. I can meet you in 3 or 4 hours. Just leave that place. I promise I will meet you."

"Where in Hanover; what hotel?"

"The….The Regal Hotel on Wilhelm Strauss Street."

"That is pathetic Sophie. There is no such hotel or street. You are going to tell me. When I start on those children in less than 5 minutes you will be screaming your whereabouts. No one is going to save them. I have been watching the place. The security guard is not due for at least half-an-hour."

The only sound was her panicked breathing.

"Ok… Ok. I am here in Assen."

His heart leaped and he gripped the phone tighter.

"Where?"

"I am just down the street. I am just 5 minutes away."

"You are lying,"

But he was sure she wasn't. He could end this now.

"I am not. I promise you."

"How do I know you are telling the truth?"

She was silent for a few seconds and when she spoke she sounded resigned.

"I can prove it. Go to the window to the left of the phone. There are two tower blocks about a half-mile away. I am on the 4th floor of the one on the left. Watch the window of the flat 3 in from the right. When you say the word I will turn the lights on and off."

He put the gun in his shoulder holster, picked up the phone and moved to the window. The wire was just long enough. He glanced at the old woman.

"If I hear those wheels move a millimeter you will regret it."

She nodded in reply. She looked distraught.

He looked through the window and saw the tower blocks.

"Ok Sophie, flash the lights."

"Ok,"

Nothing happened.

"I said do it now,"

"I just did. Where are you looking?"

"I am looking at the tower blocks. Are you pissing me about?"

He heard the panic in her voice.

"No...No I'm not; the one on the left; the 4th floor."

"That's where I am fucking looking. Do it again."

He watched for 10 seconds but saw nothing.

"I can't see anything. Did you do it?"

"Yes, you are looking in the wrong place."

But he wasn't. He was confused. Why would she lie when she knew the consequences?"

"No I'm not. You are lying. You are not fucking there are you?"

There was silence and when she spoke all the panic had gone. If anything she seemed amused.

"No, I have to admit I am not. You raped and murdered my sisters Hadyn. I will see you in hell."

She put the phone down. Hadyn stared at the receiver in amazement before he turned. His heart missed a beat as he saw the empty wheel-chair. And then it nearly stopped as his eyes mover further right to see Gertrud Rep standing with a gun pointed at his chest.

He stared into her unforgiving eyes. When she spoke her voice was cold.

"I am so glad she left one for me,"

Then she shot him twice in the chest.

Chapter Twenty-Seven

Dan heard the shots as he reached the bottom of the stairs. He took his gun from its holster and rushed up to the door with the security guard following. The door was locked. He hammered on it.

"This is the Police, open up."

He stepped back and prepared to shoot the lock but then the door opened slowly. He stepped to the side, his gun in both hands and his heart beating fast.

"You can relax Sergeant. He is dead."

Dan was stunned and relieved to hear her voice. He stepped into the hall with his gun level.

"I am in the sitting room Sergeant."

He walked in to see Gertrud standing by her chair. He saw a gun on the table. To her right, by the window, was the body of a middle-aged man. He was slumped against the wall; his white shirt covered in blood.

Dan looked at Gertrud.

"I didn't know you could walk."

"No, neither did he,"

He walked over to the body as he put the gun back in the holster.

"What happened here Gertrud?"

"He threatened to cut my eyes out. I could handle that but then he threatened to do the same to the children. I got a little angry at that so when he turned his back I took the gun from under my blanket and shot him."

"Where are the children?"

"They are with their Mother," said the security guard. "I did as you instructed Miss Rep."

"Thank-you Ronald. You can go now and can you phone the police?"

"What were the instructions?" asked Dan after Ronald had left.

"They were just to tell Heidi not to allow her children up here because I had a guest."

Dan took the man's pulse. He was dead. Without moving the body he lifted the man's jacket to reveal the gun in the shoulder holster. He looked at the phone on the floor; the receiver close to his hand.

"Is this man Franz Hadyn?"

"I believe so,"

"So he turns his back on you as he speaks on the phone. You take out your gun and when he turns round you shoot him twice in the chest. Is that how it happened?"

"Yes,"

What had she said? "I have a level of security here" He had thought she meant the guard.

"Is that a legally owned gun Gertrud?"

"No,"

"You do realize you will be in trouble."

"Yes, I guess so."

But of course it would be minimal. An SS man with a gun comes into Holland, breaks into the house of an old survivor of the Holocaust and she shoots him in self-defense. No court, especially a Dutch court, would ever convict her of anything.

"Who was he on the phone to Gertrud?"

"Sophie phoned me and he picked up."

"Where is Sophie now Gertrud?"

"I have no idea."

"I don't believe you,"

She shrugged.

"Neither did he. Would you like a cup of tea Sergeant? I am a little bit shook up. You may not believe it but that is the first person I ever killed."

"Do you regret it?"

"You would like that wouldn't you; the sweet little old lady in a wheelchair full of remorse at killing a man? It would make everything proper. No I don't regret it. I wish it hadn't been so quick. My daughter was 14 Sergeant. She was being kicked to death and when I tried to protect her, this man kicked me unconscious. How could you ask me such a thing?"

She walked into the kitchen and he followed.

"She is in Bamberg isn't she?"

"I have no idea."

"You can't protect her forever Gertrud."

She gave him a sharp look.

"Why can't I?"

"Gertrud I am a policeman. A woman is roaming Europe killing people and I know who that woman is."

"There is no way you can know."

"Gertrud if I could 100% know that no one but Ritter would be killed I would say nothing. But I can't guarantee that. Ritter is guarded by policemen at the moment. What if one of them was killed and I had said nothing."

She looked at him straight in the eye.

"You have no evidence that it is Sophie."

"Gertrud I am not going to ask when you knew that man was not a cop as the answer could incriminate you. But I think you knew from the start. You let a killer into this compound. Ronald, Heidi and the children were all in danger. The fact that Sophie was relaxed about leaving you suggests to me that you both knew his visit was a possibility. But something could have gone wrong."

"Nothing did go wrong."

"Tell me how you did it Gertrud."

"No,"

"I won't say a word, I promise. Do you really think I want to see you jailed for this?"

She looked at him and then poured the tea.

"We had a code worked out. If I left a message telling her to phone me I would answer in a certain way if there was danger. The first question she would then ask was "How did the check-up go?" If there was one SS man here I would say "They found a tumor in one lung." If there were 2 men I would have said a tumor in both lungs. I would then say they had it under control which meant I had it under control. Sophie would then get him to turn his back on me."

Dan stared at her.

"That is brilliant. Was that Sophie's idea?"

"Yes. She didn't like me being alone and wanted to hire round-the clock guards but I refused. Then she came up with this plan. The truth is Sergeant I wanted one of them to come."

"You are aiding and abetting a murderer Gertrud."

She smiled.

"I don't know anything about the other murders and I have no idea who is committing them?"

"You need to call her off Gertrud. She can't get to Ritter at the moment. If she tries an innocent person is likely to be killed."

"I suspect that won't happen."

"You don't understand Gertrud. There is no way you can be sure of that. I can't allow that possibility."

She looked at him and now she saw anger in her eyes.

"No it is you who does not understand Sergeant. You can have no understanding of what she went through. You don't know what she saw. You don't know what they did to everyone she loved. Do what you have to do Sergeant but she will never stop and I will never ask her to. If you knew the truth nor would you."

He looked at her.

"I do know the truth Gertrud. I know what she went through and what she saw. I know what she lost too."

"No you don't. You know nothing about Sophie Visser."

"I do Gertrud. I went deep into her background long before the war. She was born in Rotterdam but her Mother died while giving birth to her. Her Father killed himself soon after. Sophie was brought up by her Aunt, her Mother's sister. Her name was Gerda Janssen."

Gertrud looked at him and it was not a friendly look.

"You should stop now Sergeant. Sophie's unlucky start to life is none of your business."

"I am afraid it is my business. Gerda Janssen and her husband brought up Sophie along with her 6 daughters and 1 son. But she never changed her surname and this probably is what saved her from the rape gang. But to all intents and purposes Sophie was a 7th sister."

"I want you to leave now Sergeant."

"This does not bring me pleasure Gertrud. I would prefer to let sleeping dogs lie. But if you won't call her off I have to go after her."

Outside they heard cars pull up.

"It is the Police Gertrud. I can't lie to them. I can't let a killer run loose when I know who it is."

"You do not know. Tell them you think it is Sophie and see where that will get you. You have not a shred of evidence against her and her alibis will stand up. They will arrest her on your say-so and when she is released you will look like an idiot. All you have on her is the fact she would be highly motivated to kill these men. But so would about a 1000 others."

"You are right and I am happy to look an idiot. I have to save Ritter don't you see? No matter how evil he was, or still is, I can't just let a man be murdered when I can prevent it. But of course I don't want Sophie convicted of the other killings."

"I would ask you not to do this Sergeant."

"And I know why you don't want that but I think it would lead to a good outcome Gertrud. Sophie's arrest would make headline news across Europe. There is little evidence against her so she would probably walk free. But it would shine a light on what Ritter did to her sisters. You are a lawyer Gertrud. Wouldn't you like to bring him to court?"

She looked at him. He could tell she was torn between her professional ethics as a lawyer and her loyalty to the girl she had promised to protect so long ago.

"You have no idea what Ritter did to Sophie?"

Dan heard the policemen climbing the stairs. He sighed.

"You are right Gertrud. I don't, as you never wrote anything in your diary about her and Radcliffe had no statement from her. I know quite a bit about Sophie Visser. I know when and where she was born and what happened to her parents. I also know she was at Belsen. But one thing I don't know."

Gertrud folded her arms and looked at him as the police knocked on the door.

"And what is that Sergeant?"

"I don't know how she died."

Chapter Twenty-Eight

Private Ritter

It is Captain Hoeness. If you remember I was once your company Commander.

I will keep this as simple as possible. We have been informed by our contacts in the West German Police that it is likely that you will shortly be arrested, and probably charged, with war crimes.

The recent spate of murders concerning ex-members of your platoon has not attracted too much press attention but we have been informed that that is about to change.

The Police believe, probably rightly, that the reporting is going to be sympathetic towards the killer and biased against the victims. They believe they will be attacked for hunting down a possible victim of war crimes when the law has not punished the perpetrators of these crimes.

Whether we agree with this or not is beside the point. This is now the World we live in and we have to deal with it.

This presents a problem for us. I have to tell you that many consider that the fact that you have broken off all contact with your former comrades, and failed to financially support them in any way, means you have forfeited the right to any help from us.

However, it is not in our interests to have a media spotlight shining on us. This is probably unavoidable now but it would be hugely problematic, for possibly hundreds of us, if you were to be found guilty. It would set a legal precedent and more arrests are almost certainly going to follow.

To try to prevent this it has been decided that we will provide you with a top-class lawyer and pay all your legal costs. The Lawyers name is Gunter Keitel and he has an excellent record in cases such as this. He will contact you in the next few days.

While it would not be our preferred choice a trial could prove very beneficial to us. While it would set a legal precedent if you were found guilty the reverse is also true. A not-guilty verdict, which Keitel thinks is more likely, could mean that hundreds of SS men are free from the threat of future prosecution.

Of course you can decide to refuse our help but I have to tell you that such a refusal would not sit right with many. Their view is that it is one thing to break your oath of loyalty to your comrades but it is quite another to place those comrades in danger.

I hope you will reflect on that and act accordingly.

Yours
Captain Hoeness.

Felix read the letter for the fifth time and still couldn't decide if it contained good or very bad news. Of course it was terrible that he was going to be arrested but the offer of legal help was significant.

Gunter Keitel was something of a legend in SS circles. A devoted Nazi he had successfully defended up to 200 men both at Nuremberg and in the years afterwards. If Ritter was to be charged with war crimes there was no man more qualified to defend him.

Logically Keitel should get him off as his legal position hadn't changed since 1945. He was still a lowly private obeying orders and there were no live witnesses to the rapes. Keitel had even got Captain Hoeness off and he had been a butcher. For Keitel, clearing Ritter should be a piece of cake.

But the case was not likely to be heard for several months and during that time he would be safe as long as he didn't apply for bail. The thought of prison scared him but at the moment he was terrified every time he had to leave his house. But the killer could not get to him in prison.

He read the last few lines of the letter and his body went cold. The threat was clearly there. If Ritter didn't accept their help they were liable to kill him rather than let him stand trial.

But they might decide to kill him anyway. He was sure someone would have suggested that course of action. But, on balance, he thought that unlikely. He too could see how a not-guilty verdict could be a God-send for persecuted ex-SS men.

It would only be a temporary relief of course. If the assassin hadn't been caught in the time he spent in prison awaiting trial she would again be a threat when he was released. But, if they had got the result they wanted, the SS were likely to help him either by hiding him or getting him to South America.

It was a terrible position to be in and he was horrified at the prospect of being publicly accused of war crimes but, strangely enough, it was an accusation that could save his life.

He sat back and read the letter again. Yes, all things considered it was good news.

Chapter Twenty-Nine

In the end Dan told the Dutch police very little. He brought them up to date on the case and who he suspected the man was. He revealed why he had first contacted Gertrud and his suspicion that the hunted SS men might also conclude that she might know the killer's identity. He did not mention Sophie Visser.

They treated Gertrud with kid-gloves. They took her statement in the kitchen while scene of crime police took evidence from the body before removing it. Gertrud answered all questions calmly and without any outward sign of stress. The police charged her with illegal possession of a firearm but said there was no need for her to come to the station.

After they left she smiled at him.

"I take it you are not leaving Sergeant?"

He smiled.

"No Gertrud, I am not leaving."

"Then some more tea is in order."

He watched her move round the kitchen.

"Do you actually need the wheelchair at all?"

"I need it occasionally but it is more of a prop than anything. It is an advantage if enemies think you are weak and vulnerable. He would never have turned his back on me otherwise."

"That sounds like a line from the Mossad handbook. Did you have that gun under your blanket when I interviewed you?"

"Yes of course. He could have impersonated a British policeman just as easily as a German one. How did you figure it out Sergeant?"

"There were a number of things. Colonel Radcliffe was always very careful with his words. He said Sophie Visser was on the list of survivors. It would have been easier to say she had survived. Then there was your diary. You were scared of it falling into Ritter's hands after your death so you had to make sure he was convinced that Anna was dead if it did. You state it 3 times and this is out of character."

"You are very clever Sergeant."

"I am not anywhere near as clever as you Gertrud. There was also your description of Anna as a child. You describe her as incredibly resourceful and fearless. It is exactly how Sophie was described to me and it would certainly describe the killer."

She looked at him sadly.

"Go home Sergeant. I like you and I love Anna. I do not want to see you crossing swords."

"You know I can't do that."

"Yes you can. Your bosses wouldn't condemn you if you did. The British police do not want to catch a survivor who hunted down and killed the SS men who raped and murdered her 5 sisters. The negative publicity would be very bad. Phone your boss with those facts now. He will order you back home immediately."

Dan looked at her. She was right of course.

"You are probably right but there is still the problem of the police guarding Ritter. I could never forgive myself if one of them, or any innocent, was killed. There is also the ethical question of allowing a man to be killed when I can prevent it."

She smiled at him.

"You can't prevent it. You can make it difficult for her but you will never stop her. The truth is Sergeant that Anna promised her sisters that she would kill them all. And she will. Nothing is more important to her than keeping that promise."

"Were you speaking the truth when you said you didn't agree with these killings?"

"It is true. As a lawyer I have to oppose them and I hate to see a woman who I love as a daughter becoming a killer. As I said, I wish Anna could have enjoyed the gift of life denied to so many. And I may have been speaking the truth when I said she possibly wouldn't find peace even if she killed them all. But I am also certain she will never find peace if she doesn't."

"How did Sophie die?"

"She died the day before liberation of typhoid. You were correct in that she avoided being raped and killed because Muller didn't know she was a sister. There was a lot of confusion then and I was very ill. My friend Klara Schippers came up with the idea of swapping the identities of the 2 sisters. Ritter was still a danger as he knew Anna could convict him. When the allies collected Sophia's body we said it was Anna."

"But why did you keep the subterfuge up in the months following liberation? You had a live witness to the rapes and murders. They could have been convicted. They could have been hung."

"That was the plan. I was at deaths door but when Captain Radcliffe came to see me I told him what we had done. I could hardly speak but I made him promise to protect Anna. But a month afterwards he told us that it was still unlikely that they would be charged."

"Why was that?"

"They were still too junior. There were thousands of officers being charged and the legal system just couldn't cope. He was told by senior officers that the case wouldn't be closed but that it was way down the list of priorities."

"But surely they would have got to it eventually. It is a disgusting crime."

"You have to remember that West Germany almost immediately became the front line in the cold war. War crimes trials against enlisted men and N.C.O's were unpopular in Germany as they affected so many people. A balance had to be struck so a political decision was made to only prosecute senior officers."

"But I still don't understand why you didn't reveal Anna's real identity. Surely Ritter was no threat then."

"Yes he was and still is in fact. The decision not to prosecute lower-ranked men was never made public. No one knows what will happen in the future. If the cold war ended tomorrow the authorities might change their minds. Public opinion shifts all the time and Israel might push for more trials. If Ritter and the others knew Anna was alive they would still be a danger."

"So how did Anna feel about it?"

"She understood and agreed."

"It still feels disproportionate. Did you come to that decision out of a desire to protect Anna or because she was scared?"

She looked at him.

"Anna wasn't scared Sergeant. She stopped being scared when the first British soldier came into Belsen. We thought at the time she must be frightened. It was only later that we realized she went along with it because it suited her that they believed she was dead."

"She was 10-years-old and deeply traumatized. Surely she wasn't that calculating at that age?"

"Anna spent nearly a month hiding in a latrine Sergeant. She submerged herself in shit and piss to avoid discovery. And this was after seeing her family wiped out. Normal people can't survive that. They need a fuel and Anna's fuel was hatred. Did you think she could go back to playing with dolls? Those bastards did not kill her but Anna the child did not survive."

"Why did she wait so long?"

"I don't know really. I think maybe she just wanted to be ready. She did years of training with the Israeli's. I don't know the details but she is obviously connected to Mossad. I think she also wanted to ensure that Johannes, me and a few others were financially secure before going after them."

"That sounds like she doesn't think she will survive the hunt."

"I think she will try to survive, and stay out of prison, but only because of a sense of duty. She knows she has to look after her brother and she treats me as her Mother. But she has not had a happy life Sergeant and she doesn't fear death. In fact I think she might welcome it."

"That is incredibly sad."

Gertrud smiled.

"Yes it is Sergeant but if you ever see her again I would advise you not to mention that. Anna does not take sympathy very well."

"She told me she never got married."

"No but there was one significant man; I think he was a Mossad agent who had been at Treblinka. I don't know the details but I suspect they hunted Nazi's together for a time. But he was in a faction of Mossad that wanted to turn the focus fully on the Arab enemies of Israel and shut down the ex-Nazi operation. Anna would never accept this."

"So this is not sanctioned by Mossad?"

"It would not be sanctioned officially and I suspect agents would have been told not to help her."

"But would she get help if she asked for it?"

"I think so, up to a point anyway."

"Gertrud this is going to hit the papers in a big way. The Germans can't contain it now. The scars of the German occupation of Holland run deep. Now you have an armed ex-SS man coming to Holland and threatening a Dutch survivor of the Holocaust. It is going to be a massive story and Ritter's name is going to come up very quickly."

"So you think the Germans will prosecute him now?"

"I don't think they will have any choice as the pressure to do so will be huge. And now you have a live witness along with all the documentary evidence."

"But Anna will be suspected of killing the others. The media might not look too hard at that but the defense team certainly will. If they can prove she is a murderer it will discredit her testimony."

"It is a good point but there is hardly any evidence against her at the moment. In theory the Germans who came to London with Bauman can identify her but her real appearance is nothing like the descriptions they gave to the police at the time. But you could get a multitude of witnesses to describe

Ritter's behavior at the camp. After hearing all that the jury will believe Anna. I can't see how he won't be convicted as he can't use the "I was only following orders" plea."

Gertrud sipped her tea and looked at him for nearly a minute while she considered it.

"I agree Sergeant, it would be a good outcome and more prosecutions might follow. But there is a problem."

"You don't think Anna will agree?"

"No Sergeant, I know Anna won't agree. Anna has nothing but contempt for a legal system that allowed millions of mass murderers go free. She studied the men who raped and killed her sisters. She watched them play with their children. She watched them become rich and pillars of the community. She is outraged and genuinely bemused how it was allowed to happen. Did the lives of her sisters mean nothing?"

"But that could change now."

"It could and it probably would but even I have my doubts. The case will be heard in Germany and many there will be worried about the implications of a guilty verdict. It would mean hundreds, possibly thousands, of more trials."

"Gertrud I think this is going to be taken out of our hands. Ritter has police outside his house. After his name gets out, and I will leak it if no one else does, he will be besieged by the media. Anna will not be able to get near him and before very long he will be arrested. He will be safe from her in prison"

Gertrud smiled at him.

"You are wrong Sergeant and you don't know Anna Janssen. If you did you would know he will never be safe from her."

Chapter Thirty

"I need to know what you are going to be accused of Ritter. Your defense is obviously going to be that you were only following orders. I have to know of anything that doesn't cover. I would rather hear it for the first time now than in a court-room."

Ritter hesitated. Keitel was 72, overweight and walked with a stick but his eyes were penetrating and his voice firm. He had known he was going to be asked the question and, after long deliberation, had decided to lie. But he knew instinctively that the man would detect the lie.

"Your hesitation tells me there is something. Just answer these questions. Was it rape?"

"Yes,"

"Were there any live witnesses?"

"No,"

"Ok, that should not be a problem. Did you get that Sabine?"

The woman taking notes looked at Ritter as she nodded. "Yes I have got it,"

He saw the contempt on her heavily scarred face and looked quickly away. She hadn't spoken a word to him but her very presence made him nervous.

Keitel had phoned him the day before to arrange the meeting. After the Captain's letter Ritter had begun to worry that it was an elaborate trick by the killer to gain access to his house. In the end he had decided to meet him in a public beer-garden. But then Keitel had told him he would have a female legal-secretary with him.

"Who is she?"

"Relax Ritter it is not your killer. You might remember her in fact as she served as a secretary and a guard at Belsen. Her name is Sabine Steiner."

Ritter had recognized the name immediately but he doubted if she had ever been an official guard. She had been employed as a secretary in the main office building but, through her habit of sleeping with senior officers, she had come to wield considerable power. And she had exercised this power.

The stories about her were endless. One was that she would only have sex with an officer if he ordered 10 Jews to be killed while it was taking place. Another was that several inmates were slowly strangled to death in the same room as she had sex.

She was a die-hard Nazi and only ever wore red white and black clothes. She would walk through the barracks, looking as glamorous as a movie-star, and casually point at inmates who would then be taken away, tortured and killed.

She wasn't popular as the general view was that she was just a jumped up whore but it was dangerous to express such a view. It was well known that any soldier not showing her sufficient respect would find himself on the Russian front very quickly.

Ritter had never spoken to her or even been close to her. She seemed to take a special delight in tormenting the East European inmates and did not come into Ritter's barracks. But the glamorous sadist had held a fascination for the virginal young soldier.

But if she had been beautiful once she certainly wasn't now. Although she still wore the red blouse with white trimmings, along with a black skirt, she was now very overweight and her face was a patch-work of ugly scars. Ritter knew she had been sentenced to 10 years in prison after the war and he guessed she had been attacked there.

She would be about the same age as him but she looked much older. She had a blonde wig on and she had plastered her make-up on in a futile attempt to hide her scars. The result was an ugly, garish mess.

"I take it you have heard about Hadyn being killed in Holland," said Keitel.

"Yes,"

"Well I will tell you what I think is going to happen. The Dutch media is going to go nuts and the German investigation into the murders, or lack of it, is going to come under a spotlight. At some point I believe your name will come out. When that happens your war record is going to be published and the subject of war crimes trials is going to be raised. The media will dig up Holocaust survivors to testify against you and the police will come under pressure to arrest you. At some point they will succumb to that pressure."

"Will I get bail?"

"We are not going to apply for bail. It is safer for you if we don't."

Ritter looked at the woman's scars.

"Will I be safe in prison?"

"We will ask for you to be held in a secure unit but you will have to be careful."

"So what do I do until I am arrested?"

"We don't know for sure you will be but we will prepare just in case. Sabine will come to you with a set of questions. She will be aggressive in asking them and this is to prepare you for cross-examination. We will tell you how to answer but you have to stay in control. I will delay the case until Sabine thinks you are ready."

Ritter looked at her and then looked quickly away. He did not want this woman in his house but Keitel's tone made it obvious he would have no choice.

"If this comes out in the media I am likely to lose my job and my home."

"There is no likely about it. The school is going to come under severe criticism for employing a SS camp guard as a caretaker. But we will provide a safe-house until you are arrested."

"If you can do that why can't you get me out of the Country?"

It was the woman who answered and with some venom.

"Listen you little shit, we are not doing this for you. You are a disloyal cunt who has done nothing to help your comrades. You will do exactly as you are told or you will regret it."

"Now Sabine let us not be harsh," said Keitel. "But she is correct in that you should consider yourself under SS discipline. If things go to plan we will surely help you disappear."

"What about the police outside my house?"

"Are they checking the I.D of everyone coming there?"

"They do it the first time and then ask me if they are allowed in. I have given them a list of names. There is just my mother, my sister and a couple of teachers."

"Tell them you are expecting your legal adviser and describe Sabine to them. You will call her Sabine Krauss which is her mother's maiden name and the one on her I.D card. I suspect that they will still discover who she is but you will not use my name at all. If the media hear of my role too early it will have a negative impact."

Ritter stared at them both. How had it come to this? He had thought he was free of them. The woman especially was evil personified.

"Is there a problem?" said Keitel.

"Do we have to do this? I mean maybe all this is not needed. Maybe it would be better if you didn't help me. I could get another lawyer if needed."

"Mr. Ritter I am going to explain a few things to you. 5 members of your troop have been killed and you are probably the next target. We have absolutely no idea who the killer is. The police don't give a fuck about you. If you can get another lawyer, which is far from certain, he will defend you but he doesn't give a fuck about you either so is not going to try too hard. But we will work very hard to protect you and to clear your name. The truth is you need us."

"And if you don't accept our help we will cut your balls off," said the woman with a malevolent snarl.

He looked at them in despair. They were right. If he wanted to stay alive and out of prison he had to go along with them.

Chapter Thirty-One

The woman came the next day. Ritter watched her park her car in front of the police car and then walk to his door. He shuddered at the sight of her. The woman was so overweight the short walk seemed a struggle and sweat was making the caked on make-up run over her scarred, bloated face.

She had a black hat pulled low down her face as well as dark glasses but the scars were still very visible. Her blouse and skirt were the same Nazi colours but where once she had appeared glamorous she now looked grotesque.

The two police officers got out of the car and approached her before asking to look at her I.D Card. Ritter opened the door.

"It's alright officers this is the lady I was telling you about."

The 2 men looked disgusted as they handed the I.D. card back. Ritter didn't know if this was because of her physical appearance, her body odour or the blatant reference to the Nazi party in her attire.

They returned to their car and Ritter invited her in.

"Would you like a cup of coffee?" he asked nervously.

Her reply surprised him.

"Yes that would be nice thank-you,"

She sat down and took some papers from her brief-case as he went into the kitchen. When he returned with 2 cups she looked up and handed him a newspaper.

"The story has broken. It is front page news in Holland and will be in Germany tomorrow. So far they only have Hadyn's name and a suggestion his death is linked to several murders of former SS men. By tomorrow they will have all their names and then the media will look for the next possible target. Keitel thinks we have 2 days at most before your name comes up."

"What will happen then?"

"You will have hundreds of reporters and photographers outside your house. That is not great but a silver lining is that you will then be safe from the killer as she can't get near you. For that reason we will stay until the school asks you to leave which will probably be 2 days at the most. Then we will move you to a safe-house until you are arrested."

"Why don't we go to a safe-house straight away then I can avoid being photographed?"

"If we had suggested that straight away what would have been your reaction?"

Ritter saw what she meant.

"Yes of course, I would have suspected a trap. I would have thought you were going to kill me."

"Yes you would have done. But you are actually safer here than anywhere else. A safe-house does not give a 100% guarantee of safety. We don't know if Mossad has infiltrated our organization and we still have no idea who the killer is. The media throng will be a nuisance but the killer is never going to try to gain access to your house with them and the police outside."

"I take your point."

"Keitel can also turn it to your advantage. He can paint you as a reformed character. You have been a trusted caretaker working round children for many years. That will be a big help in court."

Ritter relaxed a little. Maybe having the SS on his side might not be so bad after all. Keitel was obviously a legal genius and the woman was being almost pleasant. He smiled.

"Yes, that is a good point,"

Now her face darkened.

"Ritter you have just fallen for an old trick. Yesterday I was abusive to you and you expected me to be the same today. When I behaved differently you relaxed. It is what the prosecuting lawyer will do. He will get you to drop your guard. That man will hate you Ritter and never forget that. He is an enemy that needs to be defeated. I will coach you and sometimes I will be nice but never forget I hate you too."

He stared at her and knew she wasn't lying. He guessed it wasn't just him. She looked full of hate for everyone.

"Ok, I understand,"

"Good so let's get started. I will ask the questions in the order we think they will be asked. I will come 3 times a day and I will test you on them. Remember your liberty and, more importantly, the liberty of thousands of SS men, rely on you answering correctly. Is that understood?"

He looked at the ugly woman he had once fantasized about. He felt deep despair and fear of the coming public exposure but it was nothing compared to his fear of the unknown assassin. It was a horrible situation to be in but this hideous woman could save his life. He nodded.

"Yes, that is understood."

Chapter Thirty-Two

Two days later Dan sat in the police car outside Felix Ritter's house and watched the gathering crowd. Ritter's name had been on the noon radio and TV reports and now, just 6 hours later, about 60 journalists and photographers were being kept from his door. In the morning, after it hit the newspapers, there would be many more.

In the end it hadn't been him who leaked the name but he was not sorry it had come out. Ritter was safe now but, in a way, so was Anna. If she couldn't get to him she couldn't be caught or killed.

It was why he had not given the German police the name Sophie Visser or Anna Janssen.

It troubled him as it was totally unprofessional. It went against everything he had been taught. However you dressed it up he was protecting a serial killer.

But already the media, especially the Dutch media, were questioning how the SS guards were able to escape prosecution at the end of the war. They would now investigate Ritter's role at the camp and encourage witnesses to crimes to come forward.

If, as seemed likely, he was arrested maybe Gertrud Rep and others could persuade Anna to appear as a witness at any trial. Such an appearance would probably mean Ritter being imprisoned for a very long time.

Gertrud had said Anna would not accept this but Dan couldn't see that she had much choice. She couldn't get at

Ritter now and, as he would be stupid to apply for bail, this would continue up to the trial.

She could wait several months until after the trial and, if he was cleared, go after him again. But Dan had told Gertrud to tell her that he could not allow this. If Anna had not put in an appearance before the end of the trial he would tell the German police that she was his chief suspect.

It was the compromise he had come up with. He would allow her to get away with the murder of 5 very bad people but he would prevent her adding a 6th.

But there was another reason he was keeping her name out of it. The SS were now involved and while he was uncomfortable not identifying her as a suspect to the police the thought of doing so to the SS was horrific.

He had first seen the fat woman in the morning before the cameras had arrived. She was an amazing sight as she waddled rather than walked to the house.

"Who the hell is that?" he asked.

The German policemen laughed.

"Quite a sight isn't she? We have christened her the Red Baroness."

"Who is she?"

"The name on her I.D card is Sabine Krauss but we have just been told that that is the name now being used by Sabine Steiner."

"Who is Sabine Steiner?"

"She is a very evil woman. She was jailed for 10 years after being implicated in the deaths of 42 inmates at Belsen. There were probably more as she is one sick woman if even half the stories about her are true. Believe it or not people used to call her the sexiest woman in the SS."

"What happened to her face?"

"There is a report that she was attacked in prison and barely survived. I would have let the bitch die."

Dan watched her approach the door. The blouse was too small and seemed ready to split at the seams. She had a black hat pulled low over her face and the collar of the blouse was turned up. But, even with the sunglasses, the scars were still very visible.

"She looks hideous."

"Well as ugly as she is on the outside she is far worse on the inside."

"What is she doing here?"

"She is working as a legal secretary. We think she is a go-between for a lawyer hired by the SS. We don't know who the lawyer is yet."

"So the SS think Ritter will be charged with war-crimes?"

"We think so and it would make sense. A guilty verdict would be bad for them but if they can get him off it would set a precedent that could make it harder for anyone else to be charged."

Dan thought about that. The SS would not know there was a live witness; no one did. If he could get Anna into the witness box she could not only convict Ritter but it would mean countless other SS men could still be charged.

"Why did she get 10 years and guards like Ritter never even got prosecuted."

"She was never officially in the SS so couldn't claim to have been carrying out orders. There was also a stack of evidence against her as she was quite brazen."

"In that case why did she only get 10?"

The policeman shrugged.

"You tell me. And she only served 6. I think she should have been executed."

Now late in the afternoon he watched her drive towards the house again. It was the 3rd time she had visited today. Because of the crowds she had to park further away this time.

A couple of photographers, probably alerted by her garish outfit, took a couple of snaps and she pulled her hat a bit lower over her face. The rest of the crowd only really took notice of her when the 2 policeman at the front of the house opened the cordon to let her in.

"So the bitch is back," said Dan to the 2 policemen in the car.

"Yes, she comes 3 times a day."

"Does anyone else visit?"

"His mother and sister came the 1st day but haven't been back since."

"How old is the sister?"

"47"

"Make sure you check her I.D."

The man laughed.

"You have a very low opinion of the German police Sergeant. We will not allow the killer to walk past us while posing as Ritter's sister."

"I am sorry it was a stupid remark."

"What are you actually doing here Sergeant? You have been here all day. Do you really think she is going to try to get to him now what with us and this crowd?"

"No I don't but my boss told me to stay. He was told by the chief that we had to maintain a presence because of the 2 killings in England."

It was only partly true.

He watched the woman ring the door-bell and then caught a glimpse of a middle-aged man opening the door. As he did so bulbs flashed as the photographers tried to get his picture.

Because of the woman's size he had to open the door wider than he would have liked but he put his hand up to shield his face.

"How long will she stay for?"

"About 30 minutes. We think she is coaching him in how to answer questions."

"Surely the school won't let this go on. How the hell did he get a job at a school anyway?"

"He obviously lied about his past. It is the weekend now but he will surely be asked to leave by Monday."

"So do you think the SS will hide him somewhere?"

"We think so if the order to arrest him doesn't come first. That of course is when he might be a little more vulnerable. The killer might try to get to him when he is moved."

He was right thought Dan. If she was mad enough to try it had to be then. And that meant she had to be close now. She had to be watching the house.

Chapter Thirty-Three

Ritter turned his back as soon as the flash-lights started but he knew they would have got a partial shot of his face. His life was in ruins. Tonight on the TV he would be headline news and tomorrow he would be fired and lose his home.

He trudged down the hall and left the fat cow to close the door. He could hear her wheezing breath as she tried to recover from the fifty meter walk from her car. But at least she didn't smell as bad this time.

"Can't you keep those fucking people away?"

Steiner did not reply. She was truly loathsome. He knew that for the next 30 minutes she would be screaming questions at him and mocking his replies. She said it was to prepare him for the trial but she obviously got pleasure from his fear and discomfort.

"I mean it. Can't you threaten them with a court order or something? I know they supposedly offer me protection from that Jewish bitch but they are going to make my life hell."

He walked into the lounge and Steiner followed.

"They are not offering you protection from the Jewish bitch Ritter."

He spun round to see her pointing a gun with a silencer at him. For several seconds his brain could not compute what his eyes were seeing. The woman was dressed the same as usual, was grossly overweight and had multiple scars on her over made-up face.

This is why it took him nearly a minute to realize that the woman was not Sabine Steiner.

He was stunned.

"Who... who are you?"

She spat out some padding she had in her cheeks and pulled her blouse up a little to show the heavy clothes beneath.

"Don't you remember me Ritter? Don't you remember fucking me when I was 10-years-old? Don't you remember being so horny that you disobeyed Muller and had another go? Don't you remember me biting your cock?"

Ritter stared at her in horror.

"No... no you died."

"No Ritter I didn't die; well not all of me anyway. I hid in that latrine for a month but I didn't die. I wouldn't allow myself to die."

Ritter tried to deny it but he knew it was true. It was the eyes. The memory of those hate-filled eyes had been etched on his brain for nearly 30 years.

"But... but they all said you had died."

"Most thought I had and the others lied."

Ritter felt the fear now. He started to tremble and felt that he could lose control of his bowels at any moment.

"Please don't kill me."

"Why would I not?"

"I didn't have a choice. Muller made me do those things. Hitler made me do those things."

"You are not being very persuasive."

"There are police outside. I will scream and they will hear me."

"If you do that I will kill you."

"You are going to kill me anyway."

She smiled.

"That is true but I expect you would like to delay your death. It is a natural human reaction. You will hope that someone will come to your aid."

He grasped at this.

"You are right. The real Sabine is due. She will be here anytime."

"No she won't."

"Have you killed her?"

She smiled

"No, I haven't killed her."

There was a silent pause after that and he couldn't afford silence.

"There are police outside and the press. You can't get away with killing me. If you go now I won't say anything."

She smiled.

"That is very kind of you."

"Please, I have a Mother and a sister."

"So did I once, actually I had 6 sisters."

Ritter was on the verge of panic but he had to stay in control.

"Can I sit down?"

She thought about it for a second then nodded.

He sat down.

"Wouldn't it be better if you let them charge me? Now you are alive I am bound to go to prison."

"I have a problem with that."

He noticed she was sweating slightly and looking uncomfortable in her layers of clothing. She glanced down and loosened her blouse and he moved his right hand behind his hip. He had to keep her talking.

"But it is better for you if I am found guilty. The SS lawyer told me so. If I am found guilty countless other members of the SS will be too. You owe it to all the victims not to kill me."

"You are lecturing me on Holocaust victims. That would be funny if it wasn't so sick."

His hand was half under the cushion now.

"There will be even more journalists outside now. The police might not be able to keep them back. They will see you."

She looked at him and then turned her back on him and walked to the curtain covered window. He jumped up and threw the cushion off the chair before grabbing the gun. He brought it to bear as she turned round; her gun by her side.

"Stay there and drop your gun?" he screamed.

She didn't drop the gun.

"You are right, there must be close to a hundred there now."

"Drop the gun or I will fire."

"You are sounding a little hysterical Felix."

"I will fire. Drop your gun."

His hand was shaking violently now. He opened his mouth to scream for the police but she saw his intention and raised her own gun.

"No shouting Felix."

With eyes almost closed he pulled the trigger.

And nothing happened.

He looked at the gun in confusion and then tried again. Again there was just the click of the firing mechanism. The woman smiled.

"It would appear your SS friend took the bullets out. She must have thought you might harm yourself."

He looked at her in horror. She was no longer smiling and he knew he was about to die. He started to cry.

"Please... please don't do this. It's not fair. I was not like the others. I had a Jewish friend at school. I was just scared. Please don't kill me. I don't deserve to die."

Her face didn't change.

"You see Felix if it was just me I would take the court option. I wouldn't like it as the memory of what happened that day, along with the month in the shit, is burned into my brain. But I might have done it for the reasons you articulated. But I can't."

He was sobbing now.

"Please, I have a Mother."

"You see Felix, I promised my sisters."

Then she shot him through the heart.

Chapter Thirty-Four

Dan watched the fat woman leave the house. It was almost dark now and the flash-bulbs lit up the area round the door. The two policemen gestured to the cameramen to let her through to her car but made no move to stop the journalists following her and shouting questions all the way.

She ignored them all and kept her head down. When she tried to drive out they blocked her exit but then the police did intervene and ordered the press pack to let her through. Dan watched her tail-lights disappear down the school road.

"It sickens me that she can strut round dressed like that."

One of the policemen nodded.

"I agree. It is pretty brazen. But what can we do? Wearing the swastika is banned in Germany but we can't ban the Nazi colours. I bet the bitch has got the swastika on her underwear though."

"Will he get any more visitors tonight?"

"He hasn't so far so I doubt it. It is possible someone from the school might come and fire him but I wouldn't expect that to happen tonight."

"So are you guys staying here all night?"

"We have another hour and then we pass it on to the night-shift."

"Ok, I will stay with you and then call it a night."

They watched in silence for 45 minutes. Dan had been on long stakeouts before when the conversation run out. He wondered if Anna had been watching the house through binoculars. It made sense and that would have meant she had seen him.

She would also have seen the fat Nazi. What would she have made of her and would she now know the SS were helping him.

Dan didn't think that was too strange as it made sense for them not to allow him to be convicted. What did surprise him was their agent.

He would have thought they would try to keep their involvement secret for a time at least. So why choose someone so open about her support for the Nazi's? It was not as if she had tried too hard to hide her identity. She was the semi-famous war criminal who had been scarred and always wore the Nazi colours. She had even stood trial in them.

Were they trying to brazen it out? Were they making a statement saying that they protected their own; that they didn't care what the rest of the world thought; they were the SS and were proud of it? But if that was the case how come the lawyer was still unnamed.

Dan felt a shiver run down his spine.

She was the semi-famous war criminal who had been scarred and always wore the Nazi colours.

He turned to the two Germans.

"I don't mean to insult you again but has anyone actually seen a recent photo of Sabine Steiner?"

They looked at each other.

"No...but it's got to be her... I mean the colours and the scars and she is too fat to be the killer."

Dan looked at them. Surely they were right.

"I really think we need to check on Ritter."

Chapter Thirty-Five

The woman was alone which surprised Dan but it had been 3 days since Ritter's murder. Maybe Johannes had already visited. He watched Anna place a flower before all 3 headstones before standing silently before the one containing the names of her sisters and parents.

He let her have a few minutes before walking slowly towards her. She cut an attractive figure in leather jacket, close-fitting jeans and knee-high boots but it was not the place for such thoughts.

Besides, while he found her attractive he should never forget that she was the most dangerous person he had ever encountered.

He moved forward while wondering how she would respond to his presence. But of course she was already aware of him.

"I take it you have not come to offer me dinner again Sergeant?" she said without turning round.

He came to stand beside her. She kept her eyes on the headstone.

"It wasn't the foremost thing on my mind, no. Hello Anna, you don't mind if I call you Anna do you?"

"No I don't mind,"

"Will you change the name on it now?"

"It will create problems and I would prefer not to but I will at some point. I owe it to Sophie. It is wrong that she is not on it. Maybe I will just leave instructions to have her name put on it after I am dead."

"Well, if you take crazy risks like you did in Bamberg that is not likely to be too long."

She kept looking at the names of her sisters.

She looked as sad as anyone he had ever seen but he knew she would never shed a tear in front of him.

"I am not scared of death Sergeant."

"I suppose I can understand that but I saw you with those children. They clearly loved you and you them. You can still choose life Anna."

"I am not saying I want to die. I am just not scared of doing so."

"It was the wrong thing to do Anna. You could have convicted him and that could have led to the convictions of thousands more."

"I know. Ritter made the same point. He even called me selfish which I thought was a bit much coming from him. I shot him soon afterwards."

"I assume I am not going to get the same reaction?"

She smiled at that.

"I think enough people have died at this spot Sergeant."

"We traced Sabine Steiner. She has been living as a recluse in a hut on an Austrian mountain. She has got a few minor scars and still wears Nazi colours but she is very thin. She hasn't left her village in years."

"I do know all this Sergeant."

"But of course Ritter and the police didn't know that. You used her reputation and went over-the-top with it. You made her big and noticeable. You also made her ugly and exaggerated the scars so that was the only thing people would remember her by."

"Was it you who worked it out so quickly? I didn't think anyone would discover his body until the next morning."

"It was what you did in London. You spent 6 months with those people but all they really remembered was the birthmark and the limp. And I didn't work it out quickly enough to save Ritter."

She didn't say anything for several seconds as she kept looking at the headstone.

"No, you didn't,"

Dan was surprised.

"Do you regret it?"

"He was just a coward; he always had been. He was weak and a follower. He did evil acts but he wasn't really evil. He raped me twice and he made me swim in shit and piss for a month. But if I hadn't promised my sisters I wouldn't have killed him. It is a strange thing but the two I hated most were him and Muller and they are the only two I have a tinge of regret about."

"I am surprised by that. Muller was an absolute monster."

"Once he was more evil than you could possibly imagine but he wasn't when I killed him. He truly regretted everything he did. He should still have been hung of course because, in his case, regret is not enough. Do you know that he donated huge amounts of money to Holocaust survival funds? He said prayers right here at Belsen."

"No, I didn't know that. It is quite a conversion."

"I enjoyed his company, can you believe that? I have tried to deny it for months because it sickens me but it's true. I actually began to like the monster that raped and killed my sisters."

"That is quite an admission. But it never stopped you killing him. Did you ever consider not doing so?"

She turned to look at him.

"No, not for an instant. You have seen his file. Do you think a man who can do such things should be allowed the time to change?"

"I was brought up to believe in redemption but if I had seen what you have seen I would almost certainly agree with you."

"But of course it was also personal. Can you imagine seeing a man hold a gun to your sister's head and then blow her brains out?"

Dan couldn't. He had read countless witness statements and he had been horrified but it was beyond his comprehension to imagine how it would have actually felt to be there. How could anyone put themselves in the place of a young boy having to kill his best friend with a shovel?

Was it even possible to imagine his Mother being stripped naked, made to carry boulders on her back and then be frozen to death on a hook.

The woman beside him had been gang-raped at the age of 10. She had then seen her sisters murdered before hiding in a latrine for a month. He knew all that and he felt sickened by it. But he couldn't begin to imagine how she felt. He doubted anyone could.

"No I can't imagine that Anna, not really."

"How did you know I would be here Sergeant?"

"I thought you would be here or in Israel. I knew you couldn't go to Assen as the police had to link Ritter's killing to Hadyn's. The sensible course would be to have gone to Israel."

She gave a little laugh.

"That is quite funny. My Mother used to say I was too practical and that Karolina was too sentimental. But now my sentimental desire to tell my sisters that it's all over has allowed you to catch up to me."

He smiled.

"I don't buy it Anna. It has been 3 days. You could have been here a day after Bamberg. I think you have been waiting for me."

Now she smiled.

"I don't suppose you will believe it is your natural charisma?"

"No I wouldn't believe that."

She gathered her thoughts before speaking.

"I wanted to know what you were going to do. I notice that my name has not appeared in the media. I owe you for that and for the fact you could have made it much harder to get at Ritter. You deserve your chance to say your peace. I take it you are here to arrest me."

"Yes I am. You have been a bloody nightmare for my career. I am never going to get promoted after you walked past a police car I was sitting in, murdered someone I was supposed to be protecting and then walked past me again."

She gave him a mocking smile.

"My heart bleeds."

He looked down at the grave and realized what a crass remark it was. He gave her a sheepish smile.

"Sorry, I am not always good at keeping things in perspective but I am good at saying the wrong thing."

She smiled.

"That's alright Sergeant. Are you always so awkward around women?"

"No, only international assassins. Will you allow me to arrest you?"

"Do you have the German Police with you?"

"No,"

"You are right. You really are not clued up about international assassins."

"I am armed,"

"Wonderful, I am sure you will get back into your bosses good books by killing a Holocaust survivor beside her family's grave at Belsen. No Sergeant I will not allow you to arrest me."

They both stood in silence for a minute. Dan wondered what it felt like to see your own name on a gravestone.

"We found a letter at Ritter's house supposedly from a Captain Hoeness. He says he didn't send it. I am guessing he is telling the truth?"

"Yes he is and Ritter did not meet a genuine SS lawyer either."

"So who were the fat woman and the guy pretending to be Keitel?"

"Now you are being silly Sergeant."

"Gertrud said you were probably getting unofficial help from Mossad."

"I hope you are not expecting me to confirm that."

"I suppose you have an alibi for Ritter?"

"Yes but I think I will wait before I reveal it."

"Fake alibi's can always be broken."

"All you could do is cast doubt on them. You won't get one member of staff at those hotels in Spain to say I wasn't there.

Even if you could it wouldn't be enough. Why didn't you tell the police in Germany about me?"

"There were a number of reasons,"

"You didn't tell them because you knew they wouldn't thank you for it. I doubt you have told your boss for the same reason. If you had named me they would have had to follow up on it. And no one wants that. Arresting assassins is normally good for a police career. But it is not the same when the killer is a female Holocaust survivor and the victims are the SS guards who killed her family."

"It's a good point and I can't deny it. Public opinion would be massively against us and you are right; the cop who instigated the investigation would be very unpopular within the police force. But none of that means I did the right thing by not telling them."

"I wouldn't be convicted Sergeant and I think you know that. You would be destroying your career for nothing."

He was silent. She was right of course.

"You have it all worked out Anna."

She stared at the headstone.

"I have nothing worked out Sergeant."

They were both silent for nearly a minute.

"That wasn't the only reason I didn't tell them."

"Oh?"

He hesitated before speaking.

"I wanted to give you a chance. At first it was just to get away. I intended to tell them but I didn't for the reasons you have mentioned. But then I wanted…"

She didn't look at him.

"Go on Sergeant,"

"This is going to sound trite but I wanted to give you a chance of life; a chance to be happy. For 27 years you have been driven by hate. You are free of them now. I can never approve of how you freed yourself but the fact remains that they are dead. You are still young Anna. You can still have a happy good life."

She said nothing for a minute and didn't look at him. Then she sort of smiled.

"You are right Sergeant. It does sound trite."

"I am sorry about that but it is hard not to be affected by your story. How you are even sane is beyond me. And even though I disagree with what you did it is difficult not to admire your determination, courage and resourcefulness."

"I believe I told you once that I am not comfortable with either sympathy or praise."

"Well, Miss Janssen I am afraid that is just tough. I do admire you and I have sympathy for what you went through and for what you lost. I am afraid you are going to have to live with that."

Her lips spread in a grin but she kept her eyes on the stone.

"You are a nice man Sergeant and that is not a sentence that passes my lips too often."

"What are you going to do Anna?"

"What will happen to the police investigation?"

"As long as there are no more killings it will wind down very quickly. It is in the interests of everyone for it to do so. I take it there are not going to be anymore killings?"

"I have no plans for any,"

"I want you to do better than that."

She smiled.

"There will be no more killings Sergeant."

"Then, after a month or so you could probably go back to Assen. Is that your intention?"

"Yes, for a time anyway,"

"At the risk of sounding trite again I hope you find peace Anna."

She shrugged and gave him a sad smile.

"I hope so too Sergeant."

"Good-bye Anna."

"When are you going back to England?"

"I am getting a ferry tomorrow morning."

She said nothing and didn't look at him.

"Why?"

"Well I was thinking you could buy me that dinner you promised me before you leave."

"I have a problem with that."

She looked at him.

"Let me guess, you don't think it is proper for a policeman to be buying dinner for a killer?"

"No, I don't think it is proper for a man on a paltry policeman's salary to be buying dinner for an incredibly rich killer. You made me look a complete idiot in Bamberg Miss Janssen. You buy the bloody dinner."

She smiled and for the first time it was a smile free of the film of sadness and mistrust.

"Ok Sergeant, I will pay the check. Do you mind giving me a few minutes alone?"

He watched her place her hand on the headstone. He knew this woman was a highly-trained killer but she now seemed almost vulnerable. He smiled.

"I will meet you by the cars,"
And then he left her to say good-bye to her sisters.

The End.

If you have enjoyed this book I would really appreciate it if you could leave a review on Amazon. Thank you.

Also by this Author

The Boy on the Beach

Jack Carter is eighteen, brilliant and driven to succeed. He and his almost life-long girlfriend are celebrating their A-level results with their friends and the future seems bright. But just weeks later Jack finds himself caught up in a violent dispute between rival gangs. It is a situation that will change all their lives forever.

Seven years later, in Thailand, an eleven year-old boy is selling ice-cream on a beach. Somchak Narong is poorly educated and his prospects severely limited. But even this bleak future is threatened when a Tsunami devastates the beach. Fighting for his life he clings to the hand of an older English girl but they are separated and the water overwhelms him.

Almost at the same time, in England, a young teacher gets engaged but, to her, the engagement seems like a betrayal. While she loves her fiancée, she cannot let go of the memories of her first love, her hatred of the men who separated them and the idea that one day they will be reunited.

She also has an unwavering conviction that the guilty men are damned and will one day suffer a terrible fate.
Five years later they begin to.
http://www.amazon.com/dp/b07hnfjrk8

How not to get ripped off by Thai bar-girls and how to have a fantastic time in the Land of Smiles
http://www.amazon.com/dp/b00xzl7uyk

Printed in Great Britain
by Amazon